Redeeming Light

Annette O'Hare

Redeeming Light
COPYRIGHT 2018 by Annette O'Hare

Contact Information: titleadmin@pelicanbookgroup.com

White Rose Publishing, a division of Pelican Ventures, LLC
www.pelicanbookgroup.com PO Box 1738 *Aztec, NM * 87410

White Rose Publishing Circle and Rosebud logo is a trademark of Pelican Ventures, LLC

Publishing History
First White Rose Edition, 2018
Paperback Edition ISBN 978-1-5223-0128-8
Electronic Edition ISBN 978-1-5223-0126-4
Published in the United States of America

Dedication

A father is neither an anchor to hold us back, nor a sail
to take us there, but a guiding light whose love shows
us the way ~ author unknown
Daddy, you will forever be in my heart.
Harrell "Jerry" McRae
1937 - 2017

What People are Saying

In Redeeming Light, Annette O'Hare once again gives us a delightful novel with fascinating characters caught up in a story of love, endurance, and complete trust in God in the most trying of times. Set on the Gulf Coast of Texas, the reader will experience the whims of the weather and tides of Bolivar and will be turning the pages to see who survives the tempest.

~Martha Rogers, author of the
Seasons of the Heart series

Annette O'Hare has nailed it in this delightful novel of a young woman's search to secure her future and finds an everlasting love. Well done!

~Cynthia Hickey, author of
the Shady Acres mystery series

1

For thou hast been a shelter for me, and a strong tower from the enemy. Psalm 61:3

Bolivar Peninsula, Late Summer 1900

Sarah Jane McKinney had dreaded the coming night for some time now. The very thought of having to deal with that crotchety old man had her stomach performing somersaults. On more than one occasion she'd heard Daddy refer to him as a shyster. And if he was brazen enough to try pulling something over on Daddy, then taking advantage of a house full of women should be as easy as drawing ants to a picnic.

"Come on, Ginger." Sarah Jane clicked her tongue and tugged the reigns. The auburn mare flipped her head in the direction Sarah indicated. The horse's russet-colored mane swished past long, dark lashes. Ginger had the glamorous eyes of a pin-up girl on a calendar. She nickered and snorted her annoyance at the restless dog running between her legs.

"Come on, Rex. Mama's gonna be angry if Maisy May gets out of her pen and eats up her vegetables, again." The keen-eyed dog snapped to attention at the sound of his name. Sarah gestured toward the gate. "Get the rope."

Eager to please his master, Rex grasped the tattered cords in his mouth and pulled. The wooden gate swung toward the scruffy dog and latched shut.

"Good boy, Rex."

The milk cow mooed her protest at being shut inside the barn.

Sarah knew firsthand that Maisy preferred the taste of Mama's homegrown produce to her store-bought feed. "Sorry, girl, but I'm not drinking any more onion-flavored milk."

With the pen secured, Ginger slowly clopped to her stall in the back of the barn. The slow cadence of her hoof falls indicated her fatigue. All the animals spent their nights in the barn except the beef stock, and Rex of course. Rex stayed in Sarah's room, much to Mama's displeasure.

Looking back, Sarah saw Maisy May's udder bag swishing to and fro as she fell in line behind Ginger. Two goats, the newborn kid, and a half-dozen or more sheep followed in step as they did every evening.

Sarah dismounted and filled Ginger's feed trough with fresh oats. Sarah unhitched the saddle and lifted it off the horse's back. She had helped her daddy take care of the ranch for years, with the help of Pedro and the other hands, but now that her father was gone she quickly came to realize how much work there really was. There were so many things that needed attention. If she didn't get some help soon, the place would fall into disrepair.

Ginger snorted her approval of dinner by plunging her long nose into the feed. Sarah brushed through the horse's fur, damp from a hard day of work. Ginger's flanks quivered with each stroke of the brush.

Without warning, Pedro stuck his head around the corner of Ginger's stall.

Sarah startled, and the goats bleated their condemnation of his intrusion. She put her hand to her chest willing her heart to slow down to its regular pace. *I need to put a bell around that man's neck.*

"I'm gonna go now, Miss Sarah, OK?"

"OK, Pedro." It was an effort for Sarah not to pick up Pedro's thick Hispanic accent. "Thanks for all your hard work today."

"I see you next week, OK? We gotta castrate those new bull before Mr. Crosby come for the herd, OK?"

Sarah draped her arms over Ginger's back. She extended a weary wave to Pedro. Exhaustion overcame her at the very thought of castrating the young bulls. It was disgusting work for sure, but she'd put it off long enough and needed to get it behind her. Her top lip curled thinking about the nauseating job that loomed ahead of them. "See you next week. Say hello to Inez for me."

He nodded. "OK." Pedro wasn't a man much for words. Having said his piece, he disappeared around the corner. He was a good man—their best man. And the only one who stayed on to help her with the herd after Daddy was killed. The others had left, afraid there would be no more work, no more pay. Not Pedro, though. He had been by Daddy's side for as long as she could remember.

But after the cattle were sold, she'd probably have to let him go too. Daddy's ranch was too big for three women and one elderly Mexican man to handle. To keep her father's MK brand alive, she'd have to scale down the operation. At least until she could get more help. Times like these made her wish she had half-brothers instead of two half-sisters.

Pedro led his mule out of the pen, where he kept

her during the day, and climbed on her back. It amazed Sarah every time his leg made it over with his diminished stature. He nudged the mule in the flanks and held tight to the homemade harness she wore. She took off down the road with a jingle from the bells around her neck, all the while hee-hawing her grievances. Pedro's wife, Inez, decorated the mule's harness with colorful ribbons and bells, making her, as she said, *"Muy bonita!"*

Sarah removed her cowboy hat, and a passel of long, blonde curls tumbled down. She shook her head and ran her fingers through the straw-colored waves. A cow lowed in the distance, drawing her from the barn. She put the hat back on and walked toward the fence.

One of the fence posts leaned precariously, demanding Sarah's attention. One more thing she needed to take care of but didn't have the time or energy for. She chose a sturdy post and leaned her weary body against it. It was the time of day she'd grown to love so much growing up on the peninsula.

The sun appeared larger than usual. It cast brilliant rays of light onto the Bolivar Point Lighthouse standing tall in the distance. The huge tower reflected the dazzling light onto the swampy pond in front of it. The water danced and glimmered. The sun gave forth its final magnificent rays before gently sinking into the waters of Galveston Bay.

The herd of fifteen hundred Texas Longhorn cattle bearing her father's MK brand grazed in the pasture. The colors of their hides were more varied than an artist's pallet. She couldn't imagine a more beautiful sight than the one that lay before her.

"Sarah Jane." Her short, red-headed mama

hollered from the back door. "Come inside and get cleaned up. Mr. Crosby will be here before you know it."

"I'll be right in, Mama." The screen door slammed shut. *Oh, Lord, I'm not looking forward to this meeting tonight. You know how Mr. Crosby is. He's not to be trusted. I need You there to make sure he doesn't take advantage of us.*

God heard her prayers, but ever since Daddy died, it felt as if He was nowhere to be found. If she was to have a successful meeting with Mr. Crosby, she needed all the heavenly assistance she could muster.

Brutus, the oldest and best of their breed stock, bellowed his long, loud cry. The cows followed him into the far pasture with a soft lowing. Mama insisted they keep Brutus after the horrible accident. She asserted they needed him to continue Daddy's near perfect line.

The broad chested king of the herd sauntered away with prideful arrogance. His seven-foot horn span swayed as he walked. Brutus was a regal animal, but it didn't matter to Sarah how majestic he might be. She turned toward the house.

She would never forget that he was responsible for goring her daddy to death.

2

Sarah and her sister, Grace, helped Mama serve up the delicious cut of beef, potatoes, gravy, green beans, fresh peaches, and yeast rolls.

Sarah paid careful attention to Mr. Laird Crosby's demeanor during supper to get a feel for how their negotiations would go afterwards. If the way he devoured Mama's home cooking had anything to do with his willingness to deal, then prosperity was on their side. But uncertainty assailed her. It seemed he'd checked his previously crotchety manner at the door. Perhaps he was on his best gentlemanly behavior since he was in the presence of ladies.

"Mrs. McKinney, that might have been the juiciest piece of roast beef I've ever tasted." Mr. Crosby patted his round belly as he followed Mama into the living room. He sat down in Daddy's chair.

Mama said nothing, so Sarah let it go.

All men were to be respected, even if they did speak with some kind of Alabama accent. He wasn't a native Texan; that much she was sure of.

"Why, thank you, Mr. Crosby. It's been a while since I've cooked for a man." Mama sat in her rocking chair and smoothed out her skirt. Rex trotted over and sat close to her. Mama put her hand on his furry head. "As you already know, our cattle provide some of the finest beef in southeast Texas—have for years now." She gestured to Sarah and her sister, standing at the doorway. "Girls, come on in and have a seat. You are as much a part of this as we are." She reached up and touched one of her faded red curls. "This will all be yours someday when I'm gone." Her voice cracked.

Sarah wanted to roll her eyes. It was Mama's new practice to voice her sense of mortality since Daddy died. She didn't buy into Mama's poor-little-old-me act. Her mother had survived a divorce and the deaths of her last two husbands. If she could live through that, then selling off a herd of cattle should be an easy day's work for her.

The middle sister, on the other hand, seemed to thrive on Mama's newfound insecurities. Most everyone considered Grace Winnie the most beautiful girl on the peninsula, with her enormous blue eyes and angelic features. Of her two sisters, Sarah was closest to Grace, but bless her heart, the poor girl was as naive as they came.

Grace rushed to Mama's side and lifted her hand. "Oh, Mama, are you getting the gloomies again?"

Mama patted Grace's arm. "I'll be fine, honey. Now have a seat." She patted the straight-backed chair next to her rocker, and Grace sat down beside her.

"Eh, hm." Mr. Crosby loudly cleared his throat. "Mrs. McKinney, even though it hasn't been clearly stated to me, I believe I can ascertain the reason as to why you've invited me out here to your ranch."

Mama raised her eyebrows. "Oh? Well, it is the spring, Mr. Crosby. And if I'm not mistaken, the late Mr. McKinney had always invited you to our ranch at this time of year to discuss the purchase of our beef stock. So naturally, I assumed the reason I invited you here was more than obvious."

"Well, you see now, that's just the thing, Mrs.

McKinney." The man turned his attention away from Mama and looked at Grace. "Darlin' would you be a dear and fetch me a cup of warm coffee and some of that delicious-looking peach cobbler I seen on the sideboard?"

Grace looked to Mama, who patted her on the knee. "Go on and get him what he wants." She left the room.

Mama clasped her hands together and leaned forward to talk to the man. "Now what was it you were saying, Mr. Crosby?"

Mama's question appeared to catch the man completely off guard as his eyes lasciviously followed Grace's backside from the room. His neck whipped around to Mama, a revolting smile on his face. "What I'm saying, Mrs. McKinney, is that, if, in fact, you have invited me here to discuss whether I intend to enter into a contract with you…*ladies*, well then, I'm sorry to disappoint you. You see, ma'am, I'm not exactly in a position to purchase your cattle this year."

"What?" Sarah jumped from her chair. "But you've always bought Daddy's beef stock. Why would this year be any different?"

Mr. Crosby tightened his jaw and sneered at Sarah. He leaned forward in his chair…Daddy's chair, and put his hand on his knee. "It's different, my dear, because you are not Clayton McKinney." He pointed at Mama and Sarah with two fingers on his right hand. "You two may be McKinneys, but you're by no means the man of the house."

Mama waved her hand at Sarah. "All right now, Sarah. Let's all calm down, and see if we can work this out." Sarah returned to her chair, and Mama turned her attention to the smug faced man. "Mr. Crosby, I'm afraid I don't understand your meaning. Of course, we're not the *man* of the house, but we're all that's left." She held up a hand in question.

He sat back in Daddy's chair and crossed his legs as though he owned the place. "I see what you're saying, Mrs. McKinney, but as far as I'm aware, you may not even be the legal owner of the Longhorn stock, since Mr. McKinney is no longer alive."

At that moment, Grace came into the living room with a steaming cup of coffee and a saucer of Mama's peach cobbler. "Here you are, Mr. Crosby." The way she politely handed them to the nasty man and even went as far as to smile at him made it obvious she hadn't been listening to the conversation. She returned to her place next to Mama.

He winked at Grace before setting the coffee on the side table. "Why thank you, darlin'."

Mama continued, a bit more frustration in her voice than before. "I'm sorry, Mr. Crosby, but how can you possibly think I'm not the legal owner of my own husband's cattle?"

Mr. Crosby took a huge bite of cobbler and didn't mind talking with his mouth full. Bits of cobbler shot from his mouth as he spoke. One of them would have to clean the floor later. "Well, ma'am, do you have any papers showing that the beef stock has been left in your name? Perhaps you are in possession of your late husband's will. Because I don't know for sure, but Mr. McKinney may very well have…say, a brother with just as much claim to the cattle as you do."

Uncle Jasper's face appeared in Sarah's thoughts. He wouldn't lay claim to Daddy's cattle and leave them penniless. He wasn't that kind of man. He was good and kindhearted like Daddy. How did this disgusting man know anything about Daddy's brother? What kind of game was he playing?

Mama looked at Sarah. She hoped her mama could find a source of support in her eyes. She turned back to her aggravator. "The only one who might have more entitlement to the cattle than I do would be my daughter, Sarah, here. As you know, she is my late husband's only heir."

Mr. Crosby picked up his coffee from the table and took a long, loud sip. "Is that right, Miss McKinney? You are your daddy's sole heir?" He wiped coffee and sweat from his lips.

Sarah stiffened her back. "That's right, I am."

Having devoured the cobbler in only a couple bites, he put the empty dish on the pedestal table next to Daddy's chair. "Well now, Miss McKinney, seeing that you claim to be the sole owner of the MK Ranch, I suppose I should be talking to you then. If you don't mind me asking, would you tell me how old you are, my dear?"

Sarah scowled at the pompous man. Righteous indignation swelled inside her. "Why, I'm seventeen and a half. Not that it's any of your business. And for your information, I never claimed to be the sole owner of this ranch. The ranch belongs to Mama."

A self-satisfied smile crept upon Mr. Crosby's face. He adjusted himself in the chair, coffee cup still in hand. "My, my, but you're just a child. How do you plan on running this ranch all by yourself? I heard about all your hands running out on you. Such a pity." The man clicked his tongue and shook his head.

Sarah flinched with every sound from his mouth. Her bottom lip began to quiver. How on earth could he know about the ranch hands leaving? Had he been snooping around in their business? Might he even have had something to do with them leaving? "Mr. Crosby, I'll have you know that we've managed to handle our affairs just fine this far." Sarah's cheeks burned. "Now, are you going to make us an offer on our beef or not?"

"All right, now. Calm yourself down, and we'll talk." He held his coffee cup out toward Grace. "Would you mind getting me another cup of coffee, darlin'?"

Sarah hated the way the man talked to them. It was typical for Grace to stay out of the conversation. She was more suited to chasing after the neighbor boy and reading the latest fashion magazines than running a cattle ranch. She was normal…not like Sarah. Grace took the coffee cup and smoothed back her long, beautiful hair. With her gaze on the floor, she silently left the room.

Mr. Crosby smiled at Sarah, infuriating her. "Well, now, I suppose I'm willing to make you all a proposition, seeing as me and your daddy were such close friends and all."

Sarah wanted to wretch. This man was never a close friend of her daddy's. He only did business with him because he always offered the most money for the cattle.

The despicable man turned his attention to Mama. "You see, June…you don't mind me calling you June, now, do you?" Mr. Crosby chuckled, causing his belly to bounce.

Mama didn't say a word, and by the look on her face, she was in shock from his brazenness.

"When I received your message, I was surprised. I found it hard to believe that you invited me—a single, and might I say, wealthy man—all the way out here from Galveston Island just to talk about...cattle."

Mama's chin dipped down, and her eyes narrowed. "Excuse me, Mr. Crosby, but what exactly are you implying?"

"Why, I think it's mighty clear to everyone here." He began to laugh softly. "What I'm saying is that when a newly widowed woman invites a man to her ranch, one can only assume she has other business in mind besides just selling cattle."

Mama shook her head.

Sarah stood, her fists clenched at her sides.

He held his hand out to Mama and chuckled. "Now listen to what I have to say, June. I have an idea in mind that would solve both our problems. It seems to me you're in need of a man who knows something about cattle. And I just happen to be a man with certain needs of my own. Now you don't want to lose your late husband's herd and his ranch too. What do you say, June? We could go to the courthouse tomorrow and make it legal."

Mama sucked in her breath and grasped at the collar of her wrap. "I'm not going to marry you. I wouldn't marry you if you were the last man in Texas!"

Grace walked through the living room door holding Mr. Crosby's coffee in her hands.

Sarah walked toward the man, her face a fiery crimson. "I don't know who you think you're dealing with, Crosby, but we're not a bunch of ignorant bumpkins like you may think! Now get out of my daddy's chair."

Grace dropped the dainty cup and saucer of coffee. The hot liquid poured out, and some splashed onto her skirt. The china shattered into pieces on the floor. She gasped and put her hands over her mouth.

Mr. Crosby got out of the chair.

Mama rose and approached the man. She moved Sarah to the side and wedged herself between him and her daughters. Anger seeped from her eyes. "Sir, I'm not the kind of woman you think I am, and you have no business coming into my house and accusing me or my daughters of anything but wanting to sell my late husband's cattle."

Mr. Crosby took a step back, almost falling into the chair. He righted himself and stuck his stubby finger into Mama's face. "Now wait just a minute there, ma'am. It's not me, but you that's out of line. Here you are inviting me, one of the most eligible bachelors in Galveston, to enjoy a lovely dinner with a house full of young, single ladies." He reached up and twisted the right side of his long-handle mustache. "Humph. For all I know, it might be you who's looking for another husband. After all, if I'm correct in my thinking, Mr. McKinney *was* your third husband, wasn't he? And to think, your poor old husband is barely cold in his grave."

Sarah could see the blood drain from Mama's already pale face.

Grace put her arm around Mama and helped her to a chair. She looked ready to faint.

Sarah could take no more. When Mama was safely sitting down, she marched to the front door and swung it open. Rex followed after her. She pointed outside and turned to Mr. Crosby. "Get out!"

Laird Crosby stomped to the door, pushing past Sarah. Before he walked out, he turned and pointed at Mama. "Woman, you better think long and hard about what I'm saying. Ain't nobody in their right mind gonna buy from a widow woman without a legal will and her brood of…of…banty hens."

It was hard to hear anything the man said with Rex barking and growling at him.

He shoved the door open the rest of the way and departed.

Sarah slammed it behind him with all her might.

Grace knelt at Mama's side and comforted her. Sarah collapsed onto her daddy's chair and rubbed the side of her face. Rex sat firmly in front of her and whimpered.

"What are we gonna do, Mama? If Mr. Crosby won't buy our stock, then who will? We'll be stuck with a pasture full of fatted cattle and no buyer."

Mama raised her head and pulled a crumpled white handkerchief from the waistband of her skirt. She wiped away her tears and stiffened her jaw. "Don't worry. I have a plan." She swiped at her nose with the handkerchief.

Sarah held her hands up in question and aggravation. She shook her head. "What plan, Mama? Don't you see we're in big trouble here?"

"Now calm down, Sarah Jane." She turned her attention to Grace. "I need you to go to the train depot first thing tomorrow morning."

Grace put her hand on Mama's knee. "Yes, ma'am. Who do you want me to wire?"

"I need you to send a wire to your Uncle Jeremiah's law office in Galveston."

Sarah breathed a sigh of relief at Mama's words. If anyone would know what to do, it would be her uncle, Jeremiah Logan.

3

Maisy May chewed her cud while Sarah sat beside her on the short, red milking stool. All the hard work she did around the ranch was worth it when it came time to sit down at the dinner table. Sarah could skip everything on her plate for one of Mama's hot buttermilk biscuits slathered with Maisy's sweet butter. Sarah whipped her head to the side, slinging hair out of her face. "Almost done, girl." Maisy May flicked her tail, mooed, and stuck her nose up in the air at the sound of Sarah's soft, soothing voice. "That's right, you're doing a real good job."

A loud clackity, clackity, clack sound startled Sarah. Rex barked and took off toward the noise.

Maisy May put her foot back, ready to move. Sarah rubbed her leg. "Steady—steady girl." One swift kick of Maisy's leg and the pail of milk would be spilled on the barn floor. *What on earth is that sound?* With the bucket in hand, Sarah headed out of the barn. She walked toward the ranch house, and it dawned on her that they had wired Uncle Jeremiah a few days earlier and he was liable to arrive at any time. Her heart and spirit leaped with the excitement of seeing her uncle. *It sure doesn't sound like Uncle Jeremiah though.*

Some of the fresh milk sloshed out of the pail when she whisked around the handrail and bounded up the two steps onto the porch that encircled the house. She abandoned the bucket, pulled open the screen, and pushed through the kitchen door.

Inside, Sarah looked at her grimy hands and then to the sink. She shrugged and made her decision. Plunging her hands into the leftover dishwater, she rubbed them together for what seemed like long enough. It had been a long while since she'd seen her uncle and didn't want to waste precious time washing to get to him. She took one of Mama's dishtowels and dried her hands. Unfortunately, she hadn't left her hands in the water long enough. Mama would be mad at how much muck she'd left on the towel. She tossed it on the counter knowing she would hear about it later, but didn't care.

Sarah went through the kitchen door and down the hall to the large family room. She was ready for the big bear hug she usually received from Uncle Jeremiah. Instead, she felt as if she'd been punched in the stomach, and all the wind had been knocked out of her. Standing in the place of her favorite uncle was her oldest sister, Louise Sullivan Culp, and her husband, Melvin Culp. She didn't even have time to wipe the bewildered look from her face.

Mama was patting Louise on the back. "There, there, now honey. Everything will be all right."

Melvin sat in one of the big overstuffed chairs. His hands were folded together and hung between his knees. The small man was bent over so much his suspenders were stretched tight. He rocked back and forth, staring at the floor.

Oh, Melvin, what have you done now? Sarah rushed to her sister's side and put a hand on her shoulder. "Louise, what's the matter?"

Louise raised her head from Mama's embrace and looked at Sarah. A steady stream of tears lined her cheeks. She made a hic-upping sound as she tried to talk. "Oh—hic—Sarah Jane—hic—it's just awful."

An unwelcomed knot swelled in her gut. "What is it, Louise?"

"It's Melvin—hic—he lost his job at the paper," she said, crying through her words.

The pain in Sarah's stomach gripped her like a blacksmith's vice. "Oh, no, that's terrible."

"And the worst part of all—hic—is that we've been kicked out of our apartment, Mama. We didn't have any money saved up to pay the rent, and they just kicked us out. We're homeless!" Louise sobbed and wailed.

Mama pulled Louise in for an embrace. "There, there, honey. Don't you worry about a thing. We'll figure this out."

Sarah's heart melted out of her chest and lay in a puddle at the bottom of her stomach. She ran to the picture window at the front of the great room. There it was, as big as Texas. Her sister and brother-in-law's wagon, parked in the front yard, filled to overflowing with all their things. The clacking she'd heard earlier was the sound of pots and pans clanging against the side of the dray. *Good grief, Melvin, you didn't even unhitch your mules.*

"Louise." Sarah turned to the sound of Mama's outburst. "You're pregnant!" Mama had her hand over her sister's belly. "And quite a ways along too. When were you going to tell us?"

Louise put her hand over Mama's. "We wanted to tell you in person…Then Melvin lost his job, and we got kicked out of our apartment, and so…here we are." Louise started her hiccupping again, and big tears tumbled freely.

"Oh, honey, don't cry, I'm so happy." Mama turned to Sarah and crossed her hands over her heart. A single tear slid down her cheek. "I'm going to be a grandma, Sarah."

Mama led Louise to one of the rocking chairs. "Now *you* have a seat. You're in the family way and don't need to overexert yourself." Her tone was beyond motherly. "And stop worrying right this instant. You'll upset my grandbaby." She turned to Melvin. "It's settled. The three of you will live here. Grace and Sarah won't mind rooming together until you get back on your feet. After all, they lived in the same room for most their lives."

Louise smiled and turned to look at Sarah. She patted her belly. "You're going to be an aunt, Sarah, aren't you happy for us?"

The question caught Sarah off guard. Of course she was happy about a baby coming into the family. A new baby was always a joyful blessing. But did the baby have to live in her home…in her room?

Sarah pasted a weak smile on her face. "I'm…I'm very happy for you Louise." She turned to her brother-in-law. "Congratulations, Melvin."

He smiled and nodded at her.

Sarah had been happy when Louise married Melvin, and they moved to their apartment in Galveston. For the first time in her life she had a bedroom all to herself.

Melvin stood and put his hands on his hips. There was no shame in his eyes. A man who lost his job and ended up on his widowed mother-in-law's doorstep with his pregnant wife should show a little humility. "Well, that wagon isn't going to unload itself. Give me a hand taking things upstairs, Sarah?"

"Um, sure just let me fetch the milk off the back porch, and I'll meet you out front." She disappeared into the kitchen and out the back door. Sarah ran straight to the barn and into Ginger's stall. The big horse whinnied when she draped her arms around her neck. She was ashamed of the fact she'd run away to pout. Grownups didn't pout, and after Daddy died Mama said she had to grow up fast. She was proud of taking over running the ranch in Daddy's absence. Then, in an instant she was a seventeen-year-old girl hiding in the barn...pouting.

"It's all settled. The three of you are going to live here." Sarah mocked her mother's voice as she spoke to her horse. "It's all settled, but I wasn't allowed to say a single word about it." She squeezed her horse's neck tighter. "Oh, Ginger, it's not fair!" Sarah swiped at a tear. "Grace and Sarah won't mind rooming together...really, Mama, because I do mind!" Anger settled over her like a dark cloud. "My daddy built this house, and I don't even get my own room!" Sarah released her horse's neck and fell back against the wall. Unlocking her knees, she slid down into a pile of hay. She wanted to give in and let the tears flow, but she was too angry.

Rex rounded the corner, his tail steadily wagging.

"Come here, boy." Comfort came in the form of wet doggie kisses. "That's just what I needed." She scratched behind his ears.

Her family didn't have a buyer for their cattle. They had two, no, three more mouths to feed and now she had to help Melvin unload all her sister's worldly possessions into her room. Sarah couldn't believe what had happened to upend her life in the course of a few days...and there wasn't a thing she could do about it.

4

The ranch house was always hot during the summer months, but with the extra people inside, the heat was unbearable. The dinner table was full even without Sarah's middle sister in attendance.

Grace had spent the day at the lighthouse. It was where she spent all her extra time, and not because she had a fondness for the old conical tower or because Mama grew up there. It was because she was in love with the young, handsome Guy Claiborne, who lived there with his aunt and uncle, the current light keepers.

Mama said grace and began passing around hearty bowls of beef stew. "This one's for Louise."

"Whoa! My goodness, Mama, that's a lot of stew for one woman." Sarah passed it along to her sister.

"She needs more food. After all, she's eating for two now." Mama was wrapped up in grandmotherly bliss.

Melvin accepted the bowl Sarah handed him. He stirred the contents and took a deep sniff. "This smells delicious, Mama June. Once again you've outdone yourself."

"Well, I don't know about all that, but thank you, Melvin."

Mama gave Sarah a bowl of stew, and then served herself. She then handed Louise the platter of warm, yellow cornbread. "Melvin, dear, will you help Louise with the butter?"

"Why, of course I will. But she's not completely helpless, Mama June. She's quite capable of buttering her own cornbread."

"I know that, Melvin, but she needs to conserve her energy for when the baby comes. Look at her, Sarah. Doesn't she just glow?"

"She's not glowing, she's sweating. We all are." She dabbed at her forehead with a napkin. "Good grief, Mama. You're acting like a silly fool."

"I can't help it. It's my first grandbaby." Mama turned her attention back to Louise. "I'm so happy you're here even if it's under bad circumstances. Now I'll know you're safe and that you're eating right. And I'll be able to help you with the birthing and caring for the baby too."

All the baby talk put Sarah off. It was too hot to eat stew and cornbread. She dropped her spoon into the bowl and pushed away from the table. "Anyone need anything from the kitchen?"

The front door swung open and slammed shut. Grace giggled, dragging Guy Claiborne by his arm into the room. The giddy look on his face said he didn't seem to mind too much. "Louise, Melvin…well, for heaven's sake. What brings the two of you all the way out here? Never mind, never mind, I'm glad you're here. I…" She started giggling again and pointed from herself to Guy. "I, we, have an announcement to make."

Mama stood up from the table. Her countenance was one of deep concern. "Well, what is it, Grace?"

"Guy has asked me to marry him, and I said yes!"

"Oh, my goodness. I don't think I can take much more news today." Mama fanned her face.

Sarah jumped from her seat and hugged her sister.

"Congratulations, you two! When's the big day?"

Grace hugged Mama's neck. "Guy and I are planning on getting married as soon as possible. What's the matter, Mama? Aren't you happy for us?" Grace sounded hurt.

"I…I…everything is happening so fast. What's the big hurry?"

"That's the exciting part, Mama." Grace pulled out a chair. "You know Guy has been waiting for a church ever since he surrendered to the ministry. Well, guess what? He's been called to a church in Tennessee, and we'll be moving there in the fall."

Melvin stood and shook Guy's hand. "Congratulations. That's great news."

Guy pumped Melvin's hand. "Thank you, we're both really happy."

"Mama…you know, me and Guy won't have a place to live until we move to Tennessee this fall. You think we could live here for a while after we get married?"

"Well, of course you can, honey. The more the merrier, I say."

Grace and Guy heard about Louise's pregnancy, and the jubilant noises started anew.

Sarah got up and went into Daddy's office. She ran her finger along the framed photo of her daddy, Grace and Louise's stepfather. The events of the past few days made her more emotional than she had been in a long, long time. "Why did you have to leave us so soon, Daddy? Things haven't been the same since you've been gone." Her chest heaved. She laid her head on her arm against the hearth. "Lord, You know I can't live here with all these people. I have to give my room up to Louise and Melvin. And now I'll have to share a room with Mama, and You know how she snores."

Rex started barking, and then four short knocks sounded at the front door.

Sarah did her best to smooth out her skirt before answering the door. Trepidation coursed through her heart. She feared Laird Crosby had returned to wreak more havoc on her family. She peeked out. "Uncle Jeremiah!" The door swung open, and she hugged him tightly around the neck. *Finally.*

"Sarah Jane, how are you, my dear?" Uncle Jeremiah barely fit through. How two people could be so different in size as her uncle and her mama and come from the same two parents was a mystery. He removed his hat and handed it to her before taking off his coat.

"I'm so happy to see you, Uncle. You sure are a sight for sore eyes." She hung the coat and hat on the hooks beside the door.

A young man stood behind Uncle Jeremiah. He was tall, at least six feet, and slender, but not scrawny. Behind his wire-framed spectacles, his eyes were the deepest of green. His slightly overgrown hair was dark as freshly plowed earth. A few wayward sprigs playfully curled around his ears.

Sarah looked away as heat rose in her cheeks.

"Sarah Jane, I would like to introduce you to my new associate, Frederick Chessher."

Mr. Chessher held his hand out to Sarah. "How do you do, ma'am?"

"Pleased to meet you, Mr. Chessher." She gestured to the couches. "Won't you both have a seat while I fetch the others?"

Sarah stopped in the hall and leaned her head back

against the wall. She put her hand to her chest and released the air she'd been holding in. All the problems that had overwhelmed her only moments before faded into the distance. Sisters, brothers-in-law, babies, cattle, none of it mattered right now. There was no place in her mind for such things, having just laid eyes on the most handsome man she'd ever seen in her entire life. She let his name roll off her tongue. "Frederick Chessher."

5

Jeremiah Logan set his coffee mug down on the table and turned to Mama. "So, you said in your wire that Laird Crosby wasn't very gentlemanly with you?"

Sarah smoothed out her skirt. She was never so glad as when Louise and Melvin excused themselves to start unpacking their things—even if it was into her room. And when Mama didn't argue with Grace and Guy when they left for the lighthouse, Sarah felt as if she'd won another victory. She wanted to get to know Mr. Chessher.

Mama tugged at the collar of her blouse. Her voice revealed the anguish she felt. "Oh, Jeremiah, he had the manners of a boar hog. He implied that our cattle might not even belong to us since Clayton didn't have a will. He said that Clayton's brother, Jasper, could have as much claim to the cattle as we do. And not only did he refuse to buy from us, he tried to make a trade with me." Color rose in her face. "He implied that if I didn't marry him and take care of his…his needs, that I might lose the cattle, the ranch, everything. Can you believe the gall of that man?"

"That man is a…" He didn't finish his sentence. "Don't worry about Jasper taking your cattle. He's so wealthy he has no need of it, and besides, he's not entitled to it anyway."

Sarah stole glances at Mr. Chessher.

He pulled at his collar, and his cheeks were

turning red.

Is he upset like Uncle Jeremiah, or am I making him uncomfortable?

Mr. Chessher extended a hand toward Mama. "Mrs. McKinney, if I might ask, why not simply find another buyer for the cattle? Surely there are others who would be interested in the stock if it's as good as Mr. Logan claims it is."

"We've tried," Sarah said. "There are only a couple hundred people on the entire peninsula, and most of them are farmers. Everyone we've inquired with locally has the sale of their own cattle to worry about and can't be bothered with helping us sell ours."

Mama wrung her hands together. "She's right, Mr. Chessher. We've spoken to every rancher on the peninsula, and no one is willing to help us."

Uncle Jeremiah rose from the sofa and rested his elbow on the fireplace mantel. Rubbing his finger along the edge of a candleholder made from a deer antler, he stared at them. "I'm still trying to figure out a way to get back at that dog, Laird Crosby. But let's put our heads together and figure this out."

"For the love of Pete, this is 1900." Mr. Chessher gestured about the room. "There must be countless options for selling off this herd. How about the rail? Why not load the cattle on a train and ship them up north, or even out west? I understand buyers are paying top dollar for Texas beef."

Sarah stared at Mr. Chessher in complete admiration. She put her hand to her collar and sighed. His eloquent New England speech enamored her. She was embarrassed for him to hear her south Texas drawl.

Uncle Jeremiah walked over to the sofa. He stared

at Mama as if a firework had gone off. "June…I'm surprised you didn't think of that. Your second husband's brother, Mr. Winnie, headed up The Galveston and Interstate Rail. He's been in on it from the beginning. Surely he'll help you move the cattle out."

"That's a good idea and all, but it doesn't solve the problem of who'll drive the cattle to the High Island terminal."

Sarah traded looks between Mama and Uncle Jeremiah. "I don't understand what the big problem is. We don't have to drive the cattle all the way to High Island. We can load them up right here at the Bolivar Station."

"No, honey, we can't." Mama pursed her lips. "You know our little station isn't used to load cattle. We would have to drive the entire herd up to the High Island stock pens. That's our only choice."

Mr. Chessher spoke up. "Perhaps Mr. Logan could post an advertisement for some cattle drivers who could move the herd to High Island."

Uncle Jeremiah and Mama exchanged looks between one another, nodding in agreement.

Mama leaned against the arm of the chair where Sarah sat and put her arm around her shoulders. "I'm getting too old for all this."

"You're getting too old for what, Mama?"

"For all this. The land, the cattle." Her face held a pained expression, her voice mournfully soft as she gestured toward the cattle outside grazing in the field. "This old ranch house. It's more than we can take care of."

Uncle Jeremiah gave his sister a disparaging look. "Now, June, you're acting a bit overdramatic. You and the girls have been through a lot over the years. But you're not old, and we don't need to worry about everything all at once."

Mama stood straight and tall. "I beg your pardon, Jeremiah Logan, but I'm not being dramatic. I'm nearly forty-one years old, and…and that's too old to be running a cattle ranch. Besides, I'm not interested in raising cattle anymore. That was Clayton's business, not mine. When this herd is sold off, I'm selling the breed stock and be done with it. I don't want anything to get in the way of me caring for my grandbaby when it gets here. Except for maybe a small boarding house. I've been thinking about turning this ranch into one."

So now the truth comes out!

"How could you? The cattle and this ranch are the only things we have left of Daddy, and you want to sell them off without a second thought. What about his legacy, Mama?" Sarah pointed to the hand-crafted wrought iron MK brand embellishing the stone fireplace as tears ran down her cheeks. "Don't you even care about keeping the family's brand alive? Because I do."

Mr. Chessher took a handkerchief from his pocket and offered it to Sarah. "Here you are, ma'am."

Sarah dabbed at her eyes. "Thank you, Mr. Chessher."

Uncle Jeremiah held his palms out. "All right ladies, let's all calm down and talk things out. First, we need to hire a cattleman to drive the herd to…"

"I'll do it." Every head in the room turned toward Sarah. She looked Mama straight in the eye. "I'll drive the herd to High Island, and I want to continue raising the McKinney brand too. Even if you don't, Mama!"

Uncle Jeremiah watched in amazement.

Mr. Chessher revealed a look of contempt.

Women probably weren't allowed to speak their minds where he came from. She sent a half-smile his way. *Welcome to Texas!*

"I'm so sorry, Sarah Jane. I wasn't thinking about anyone but myself. I never thought about you wanting to continue working your daddy's ranch. It's hard work—man's work, but I know how much you loved him…we all did, and if you want to keep raising McKinney cattle then you should go right ahead. Can you forgive me, baby?" Mama held her arms open.

Sarah went into her embrace. "I forgive you, Mama."

Uncle Jeremiah clapped his large hands. "Well, then, that settles it. Sarah Jane will drive the cattle to High Island. With an escort, I might add, and then continue raising the McKinney brand."

"Yes, sir. I promise I'll have a proper escort. And Mama, I don't know how to say this in a nice way, but I'm not staying here to help you run a boarding house. Maybe you and Louise and Melvin can do that. I need my own place with people who know what they're doing."

"I don't know what you expect me to do about it, young lady. I'm not kicking my daughter and her husband out while she's pregnant with my grandbaby. And Grace and Guy don't plan on staying here but a few months after they get married."

"Of course they don't plan on it, but you know how things like that usually go. A couple months can turn into who knows how long."

"All right, now let's think about this a moment." Uncle Jeremiah looked at Sarah. "You want to raise your daddy's cattle, but not as long as you have to put up with your sisters and their husbands."

Sarah bowed her head and traced a pattern on the carpet with her foot, embarrassed. "Well, they're not really that bad—they just don't know anything about raising cattle."

"And you don't want anyone leaving the roost, especially not Louise and that grandbaby." Uncle Jeremiah looked at Mama for confirmation.

"No, not really. Of course I want to be close to my grandbaby... I want to be close to all my children. That's why I wanted to start a boarding house. But I suppose not everyone is favorable to that idea." Mama's words were curt.

"I think I have an idea." Uncle Jeremiah extended his hand to Sarah. "Why don't we make plans to ship your father's breed stock to my ranch up in Houston? After you drive the cattle to High Island, of course. It won't be too much of a burden on my people, and you'll have time to plan what you'll do next."

Mr. Chessher put his hands together. "Wonderful. It sounds as if you've come up with a plan that will please everyone."

"Then it's settled. I'll start making the arrangements tomorrow." Sarah was grateful.

Uncle Jeremiah retrieved his coffee mug. "You have any more of that coffee, June?"

Mama headed toward the kitchen with her brother close behind.

Sarah was left alone with Uncle Jeremiah's handsome young associate. "Would you like some coffee, Mr. Chessher?"

He seemed caught off guard. "Um...certainly. Miss McKinney, I realize I don't know much of anything about cattle, but I would like to offer you my assistance if there's anything I can do to help you."

Sarah touched the lace on her bodice. "Well, thank you kindly, Mr. Chessher. I just might take you up on your offer." His smile made her knees weak, and it felt as if someone had poured warm caramel down her back. She walked to the kitchen before they gave way completely. Mr. Chessher probably had no knowledge of how to raise cattle, but she would gladly take on the challenge of teaching him everything she knew.

6

Sarah picked up the heavy bale of hay and hefted it onto the wagon. She wiped her forehead with the back of her arm and let out a long puff of air. *Thank goodness Daddy never bought hay bales any heavier than these.*

Grace, the petite one of her two sisters, scooped a small patty of horse dung onto a shovel, grunting and groaning all the while.

Sarah rolled her eyes and turned just in time to jump out of the way of a bale of hay crashing down beside her.

"Is that enough, Sarah?" Melvin hollered from the hayloft.

"Yes, that will be quite enough."

"Good, that's hard work." Melvin climbed down the ladder and stretched.

Sarah loaded the last bale onto the wagon and dipped a cup into the water pail.

Melvin picked up the pen and paper he'd brought out, and Grace scooped up some water for herself.

"Hey, whatever happened to the money your daddy set aside for you to go to Bible College in Indiana?"

Grace smiled over the top of her water cup. Her soft eyes revealed the happiness in her heart. "We've decided to save it so we can buy a house when we get to Tennessee. Guy wants to start a family right away."

Her cheeks colored red, and she changed the subject. "Look at Melvin over there. What do you think he's writing?"

"Hey, Melvin, what are you writing there?" Sarah called out to him.

"Oh, it's a sonnet for Louise. She hasn't been feeling well with the pregnancy, and I'm hoping this will cheer her up. Besides, I must keep my writing skills honed for when I get another job."

Grace sat down beside Melvin, and they began discussing writing instruments.

Sarah tuned out. There was a cattle drive to plan and breed stock that needed to be shipped to Houston. And she needed her own place if she was to continue raising the McKinney beef stock. She threw her cup into the water pail with a splash. "Melvin, we're done for today. But tomorrow I need you to work with Pedro while I'm gone."

"But, but I need to start working on…"

"No buts. If you and Louise are living here, then you have to help out."

"All right, fine. You're right, I suppose."

"Just do whatever Pedro tells you. He's a good man, and he knows what needs to be done."

"And just where do you think you're going tomorrow?" Grace asked.

"I'm going to Galveston. I'm leaving tonight."

"If you think Mama will let you go to Galveston by yourself then you've lost your mind, baby sister."

Sarah walked to the house without answering her sister. She dumped her muddy work boots near the door. After she'd washed up and changed her clothes, she threw a few things into her travel bag. She brushed out her hair and tied it back before putting on a green hat that matched her skirt. After buttoning up her black boots, she slid her money purse into a pocket sewn inside her skirt. She rummaged in her bedside drawer, found her derringer, and rubbed the shiny silver scrollwork on the barrel of the small gun Daddy had given her when she'd turned fifteen. The pearl handle fit perfectly in her hand. She dropped it inside a reticule with a handful of bullets and snapped it shut.

A few minutes later, her hand was on the front door, ready to make her escape. The smell of fried chicken wafted through the house. Oh, how she hated to leave on fried chicken night, especially when her stomach was empty. "Mama, I'm leaving now. I'll be home tomorrow evening." She pulled the door open.

Mama rushed into the room, her eyes full of questions. "Where are you going? What do you mean you'll be home tomorrow evening? You didn't ask me if you could go anywhere."

"I'm headed to Galveston to talk to Uncle Jeremiah about the cattle drive. I'm hoping he can help me find a few riders."

Louise, who'd followed Mama, put a hand on her belly. "You could ask Melvin to help you move the cattle. He knows how to ride a horse."

"Oh, that's all right, Louise. Melvin needs to stay here and watch over all of you. Besides, it'll take someone with experience to move the herd."

"I suppose you're right." Louise rubbed her middle. "But Sarah, you don't have any experience moving cows, either."

"Yes, but I know how it's done. So…I guess I'll be going now."

"I don't think so, young lady." Mama was firm. "You will not be going to Galveston without someone to chaperone you."

"Mama…if I don't hurry, I'll miss the ferry."

"Grace or Melvin…pick one." Mama's arms were crossed. She meant it.

Sarah huffed out a loud breath. "Grace."

The ferry waited at the dock.

Sarah and Grace made it with time to spare.

Grace was none too happy when told she had to clean up and pack a bag so she could escort her sister to Galveston, and now she complained of being sweaty from their dash to the boat. Her hair had fallen, and she fussed as she put it to rights.

Mama had packed a basket of fried chicken with other goodies, which made Grace stop huffing as they delved into it.

Sarah's mind drifted to one Mr. Frederick Chessher. She wished he had reason to take his spectacles off so she could get a better look at those green eyes. They were brilliant, even behind the thick glass. And someone needed to give his hair a good trim. It was so out of control, the way it playfully twisted around his ears. She sucked in a deep breath and cleared her mind of the tawdry thoughts that tried creeping in. *I wonder if Grace ever has thoughts like that about Guy Claiborne? Oh, Sarah Jane McKinney, what's come over you?*

She pulled a hanky from a puffy shirtsleeve and dabbed at her misty forehead. It was time she got her mind off Mr. Chessher and concentrated on her mission. The ferry had left the dock and was well on its way to Galveston Island. The ride wouldn't give her near the amount of time needed to make up a good reason for her visit to Uncle Jeremiah's firm. And with Grace chattering on about wedding dresses, flower bouquets and such, she had even less time.

The lighthouse beamed until the last of its rays faded into the distance. The comforting beacon guided ships safely to Galveston's port. Mama told her it had been there long before Sarah was born and it would probably continue protecting the coast after she was gone.

Sarah longed for something so reassuring and enduring in her own life. The ferry bobbed up and down. She wished the swells would abate before she lost her supper. Something tugged at her heart. God was trying to garner her attention. *Yes, Father, I remember. Thou rulest the raging of the sea. When the waves thereof arise, thou stillest them.*

The words in the eighty-ninth Psalm had been emblazoned on her heart since childhood. God had always been the constant in her life. Even when Daddy died, He had been there to help her carry on. He had never left her or forsaken her. Now she had to trust in Him to complete the undertaking that was before her.

7

Strand Street in Galveston bustled with activity. There was an air of pride in the townspeople, fitting for the largest city in Texas. The town boasted eighteen newspapers and the largest cotton port in the nation. Anything new or noteworthy in the field of technology was generally first reported in Galveston.

Sarah and Grace moved through the crowd of people at a quick pace.

Uncle Jeremiah's law office was just up ahead.

Sarah wished her sister wasn't there watching her every move. But if she had to have an escort, she preferred Grace to Melvin…even if her sister had kept her up all night talking about her precious Guy. Sarah pushed the door open. A little bell tinkled. Uncle Jeremiah's law office had a smell of paper and ink.

Frederick was standing beside a large oak desk looking as handsome as ever. Seated behind the desk was a beautiful young woman with shoulder-length curls. They seemed to be talking about the papers she held in her hand.

The look on Frederick's face disheartened her. He didn't recognize who she was. Her first instinct was to grab Grace by the hand and run back out the door. If he didn't remember her, then she obviously hadn't made the same impression on him as he had on her. Now was as good a time as any to cut and run. She backed up a step and bumped into Grace.

"Miss McKinney, what a surprise. Whatever brings you to Galveston?" He walked toward her and smiled. "Mrs. Gilley and I were just wrapping things up here. What can I do for you two ladies?"

Sarah offered her gloved hand to him.

He shook it gently before shaking Grace's outstretched hand.

Mrs. Gilley loudly cleared her throat, commanding Frederick's attention.

Frederick turned to the young woman. "Oh, please forgive me. Miss McKinney, Miss Winnie, allow me to introduce Mrs. Gilley, our resident secretary, and bookkeeper."

Mrs. Gilley approached Sarah and Grace and shook their hands. "How do you do? So nice to meet you."

Sarah was happy for the interruption. It gave her just enough time to think of something to say since being in Frederick's presence made it hard for her to form intelligible sentences. "Yes, Mr. Chessher, I've come to talk to Uncle Jeremiah about the cattle drive. Is he in his office?"

Frederick dipped his head to the side, a pained look on his face. "Why no, I'm sorry, but your uncle has been called out of town on business. I'm afraid he won't be back for a few days yet."

"Oh." Sarah had hoped Uncle Jeremiah would be out of town, but never dreamed it would actually happen. She found herself at a loss for words. "Then I suppose…"

"Mr. Chessher, would you care to join my sister and I for lunch?" Grace blurted out her question, cutting Sarah off mid-sentence. She caught Sarah off guard, but Frederick looked surprised too.

"Uh…of course. I'd love to accompany you two ladies to lunch. It will be my treat." His eyes began to twinkle. "Have you ever had German cuisine?" Frederick removed his hat from the rack and popped it down on his head. He offered his elbow to Grace, and she looped her arm through his. He then offered his other arm to Sarah, and she took hold of it.

The trio made their way down Strand Street.

Grace chattered away about every single thing she saw in the shop windows. Of course, everything she saw gave her a new idea for her wedding.

Sarah was satisfied to hold onto Frederick's strong arm and walk in silence by his side.

~*~

Frederick helped both ladies into their seats, and then sat down across from Miss McKinney. The restaurant wasn't the nicest in town, but it was one of his favorites. He hoped the smell of freshly boiled German cabbage wouldn't be an affront to their noses. He had developed a craving for the fare since coming to Galveston and trusted they would too.

"Well then, isn't this lovely?" Miss Winnie took her napkin from the table and slid it onto her lap. "The three of us having…German food. Should be quite an experience, I'm sure."

Frederick smiled. "I apologize for the strong smell, Miss Winnie, but I assure you, you'll love the food here."

Miss McKinney picked up her napkin and looked at Frederick. "It's really not so bad, Mr. Chessher. I love cabbage."

"Wonderful, but it's sauerkraut. And please, call

me Frederick."

"All right…Frederick." He noticed color appearing to rise in Miss McKinney's cheeks upon saying his name. It caused him to wonder, but he let it pass.

The waiter approached the table and set glasses of water before them and left again.

Frederick opened his mouth to speak.

Miss Winnie suddenly gasped and drew her hand to her chest. "Oh, my stars and garters!"

Miss McKinney grasped the table and looked at her sister with wide eyes. "What is the matter with you? You scared me half to death."

Miss Winnie raised her hand. "I've just remembered that I left my reticule in the hotel lobby."

"No, you…" Miss McKinney tried to speak, but was cut short by her sister.

"Yes, yes. I must go directly and retrieve it." She backed her chair away from the table, and Frederick stood. "I can't believe what a silly nilly I am. I'm so sorry, Mr. Chessher. You will take good care of my little sister, won't you?" She held her hand out to Frederick.

Befuddled, he shook her hand. "Well…yes, of course."

"All right then, I'll be going now, and don't wait for me. There's a shop we passed along the way that I simply must go in and browse. I'll meet up with the two of you at the law office."

Frederick saw a strange look pass between the two sisters. He contemplated whether this had all been set up beforehand. Miss McKinney's bewildered stare at her sister told him otherwise. Then Miss Winnie turned and breezed out the café door.

The waiter returned with a pad and pencil in

hand. "Youse two ready to order, or we gonna wait for the utha lady to get back?"

Frederick winced at the waiter's grinding New England accent. His parents wouldn't dream of allowing their progeny to speak in such a manner. "No, I don't believe she's coming back." He looked to his companion. "Miss McKinney, would you care to order?"

"Would you mind ordering for me, Frederick? I haven't a clue what to get."

He gave her a smile. "I'd be glad to." He turned to the waiter. "Two specials, please."

"You got it." The young man made a scribble on his tablet, tucked the pencil behind his ear, and walked to the kitchen.

Frederick gave Miss McKinney his full attention. "I certainly hope you'll like the food. It's one of my favorites—so hearty and down-to-earth. So different from the food back home."

"So tell me, Frederick, where is home?"

He leaned back in his chair. "Hartford, Connecticut...many miles from here, I'm afraid."

Miss McKinney bent her head to the side and one of the blonde pin curls she'd fastened to the top of her head carelessly fell. She put it back in place as she spoke. "Oh, do you miss your family?"

Frederick became reflective. "Yes, I miss Mother and Father, but mostly my two little sisters. And of course, my brothers at Phi Delta Phi."

"I don't understand. You have what kind of brothers?"

He chuckled. "Not real brothers, of course, although they are close as blood to me. They're my fraternity brothers from Harvard Law School in

Cambridge. A lively bunch they are!"

Miss McKinney's eyebrows rose as she challenged him. "Oh, I see. So can I assume that your sisters are real sisters?"

Frederick enjoyed her forthright way of speaking. "Yes, of course they are. Elizabeth and Mary are their names."

"Your sisters both have biblical names. Why didn't your mother name you after someone from the Bible?"

He blinked, caught completely off guard by her question. It had never occurred to him that Elizabeth and Mary were Bible names. He furrowed his brow and shook his head. "To tell the truth, I'm not exactly sure. My father has never been much of a church-going man. Of course, Mother insisted we go on the high holy days. I suppose I don't have an answer to your question."

Miss McKinney's hand flew to her chest. He hoped it hadn't been what he'd said about church. He knew her uncle was a church-going man. It simply hadn't been of much importance to his family. He was quick to change the subject. "So now you know all about me…tell me about yourself."

~*~

Sarah had to collect herself before her countenance betrayed her feelings. She couldn't imagine what kind of family didn't attend regular Sunday services. That would have to change if she was to have anything to do with him.

"Well, I suppose you already know about my two sisters. Grace is engaged to be married. And there's my sister, Louise and her husband, Melvin Culp. They're going to have a baby. It's their first." Sarah worked up the courage to look into those handsome green eyes. She had no idea where it came from, but she leaned her head to the side, gave a demure smile, and batted her lashes at him.

"Are you all right, Miss McKinney? Is there something in your eye?" Frederick began digging in his pocket. "Here, use my handkerchief."

She snatched the hankie and put it to her eye before he realized what she had done. The heat rose in her cheeks. "Thank you. I'm fine, really." She tried to hide the blazing inferno creeping up her face behind the small cloth.

"Well isn't that exciting. Your mother must be overjoyed." Then Frederick did the worst possible thing. He touched her hand where it rested on the table.

Sarah sucked in her breath, and her eyes grew wide.

"About the baby, I mean. Your mother is ecstatic I'm sure."

Sarah's heart pounded wildly. The feel of his warm hand covering hers was simply delightful. *Get hold of yourself, Sarah. He's just a man, for heaven's sake. A dreamy, handsome, eloquent speaking man with eyes the color of polished emeralds.*

"Are you sure you're all right, Miss McKinney?" Frederick withdrew his hand "Your face is positively glowing."

Her hand went to her cheek. She had to think of something quick. "Oh, heavens, I just get so emotional when I think about that little baby coming into our lives. Don't you think babies are such a blessing?"

Frederick's mouth turned down at the corners.

"Well, I...." He stopped speaking when a steaming plate of German sauerkraut and sausages was placed before him. He picked up his fork. "Ah, here we go."

Sarah huffed out a breath as tension melted. She'd never been so happy to see a plateful of kraut and sausages.

8

Miss McKinney hadn't eaten much of her lunch. Frederick regretted bringing her to the small diner, and for sauerkraut, no less. Nothing was more of an offense to the senses than fermented cabbage. What would her uncle think of his choice? Frederick had the feeling Miss McKinney might have been flirting. It was imperative he not give her a reason to think he was interested. But gazing at the gorgeous, blonde-haired, blue-eyed beauty proved difficult. Frederick made small talk while they ate. "I'm sorry I don't know very much about cattle drives…or cattle, for that matter. I wish there were more I could do to help. What exactly had you planned to discuss with your uncle?"

Miss McKinney looked up to the ceiling as though the answer to his question might be found there. "Oh, well I, uh…a trail boss. I need to hire a trail boss."

Frederick raised his brows. "A trail boss…I see. And how does one go about acquiring a trail boss?"

"Yes, that's the question of the hour, isn't it? I was hoping Uncle Jeremiah would help me with an answer, but I suppose that won't be happening."

"Oh, yes, well I'm quite sorry. I'm afraid I've been no help at all."

Miss McKinney's eyes fluttered, and her hand moved toward Frederick.

He wanted to fold his hands in his lap, but that would have been entirely too rude. Having no other choice, he allowed her to touch his hand. It was all he could do to suppress the feeling marching up and down his spine.

"Don't worry, Frederick. I'll figure this out on my own. I can be very resourceful when the need arises." She patted his hand. "And thank you so much for treating me to lunch."

Frederick wiped his hands on his napkin. "You're very welcome. Your company was my pleasure." He tossed the napkin on his half-eaten meal. "Are you ready to go, then?"

Her head jerked back, and her shoulders slumped. "All right, we can go."

"Very good." Frederick bounded from his seat and moved to help with her chair. "Here we go." He left coins on the table and rushed her out the door. He hated to be rude, but he needed to distance himself from the vexing vixen before his mind wrote a check that his heart couldn't cash.

~*~

Sarah considered herself somewhat perceptive, but she couldn't understand what was going on inside this man's head. He obviously couldn't tell when a young lady was interested in him. And why did he rush her out of the diner so quickly? And if he didn't slow his pace she would have to run to keep up. "Frederick, Frederick, can we please slow down?"

Frederick stopped and turned. "I do apologize, Miss McKinney. I sometimes forget how briskly I walk. Must be a carryover from my days on the Harvard track and field team."

Sarah caught up. "If that's your walk I'd hate to

see you in a hurry!"

Frederick chuckled. "The office is just up ahead." He pointed up Strand Street.

Sarah offered her arm. He acted as though he didn't know what to do. *OK, Mr. Frederick Chessher. This is your last chance. Take it or leave it.*

With what appeared to be trepidation, Frederick hooked arms with Sarah, and they walked much slower down the street. Upon reaching her uncle's law office, he opened the door and ushered her to the group of overstuffed chairs in the lobby. Sarah sat in the cozy loveseat and folded her hands in her lap.

Tension melted from Frederick's shoulders when Mrs. Gilley stepped out and walked toward her desk holding a cup of steaming liquid. "Oh, Mrs. Gilley, thank goodness you're here."

"But I've been here all day, Mr. Chessher. Is there something you need?" She set the cup on her desk, her expression puzzled.

"Um…yes, would you mind pulling the um, the um…the Garner file? Yes, that's it." He snapped his fingers as if he'd just remembered.

Mrs. Gilley's brow furrowed. "The Garner case was closed over a year ago. Has something come up?"

Frederick looked befuddled. He spoke curtly to the woman. "Not yet, but I'm certain it will. Now please retrieve the file for me."

"Yes, sir." Mrs. Gilley huffed out a breath and left the room.

"Won't you come sit?" Sarah patted the chair.

"Um, yes, of course." Frederick sat next to her, but didn't make eye contact. He fidgeted with a button on his coat.

Sarah reached over and held his hand still. "What

on earth is the matter with you, Frederick?"

He slumped back and pulled his hand away. "I must be honest with you, Miss McKinney. I have a lady friend in Beaumont, Texas and I beg your pardon, but she would interpret our hand holding as entirely inappropriate." Frederick averted his gaze and straightened his tie. "And…in all honesty, you have become quite the distraction to me."

A flood of heat rose up Sarah's neck. Had she been at home, a statement like that would have brought about a flurry of condemnation. Sarah rose from her chair. "Excuse me, Mr. Chessher, I'll be going now. I, I need to find out what's happened to my…"

Frederick leaped from his seat nearly knocking Sarah off her feet. "Please, Miss McKinney, don't be offended by what I said. What I meant is that…"

The bell tinkled, and Grace pushed open the office door.

"Oh, look, Grace has found her way back." Sarah grabbed her sister in a bear hug. "I'm so glad to see you. I was worried something terrible had happened to you."

Grace squinted at Sarah as if a complete stranger had embraced her. "Um, no, I'm fine, except for feeling addle minded for forgetting my reticule." She held up the small bag. "But I have it now. Shall we sit?"

Sarah quickly cut her off. "Oh, Grace, you aren't addled, you're just confused."

Frederick's scrutiny landed on Grace. "What is it you're confused about, Miss Winnie?"

Grace, in turn, tented her eyebrows and looked directly at Sarah. "Why I'm not exactly sure, Mr. Chessher. Sister, can you apprise the rest of us about what it is exactly that I'm confused about?"

Sarah patted Grace's arm. "Now, sister, you said yourself that we have a lot to do to get ready for your wedding. We can't stay here all day dilly-dallying."

Sarah took Grace's elbow and gently nudged her. "Come on now, let's go."

Grace yanked her arm from Sarah's grip. "But I just got here!"

Sarah's chin quivered. "And now we're going."

Grace's eyes held empathy, and she gave a sympathetic nod. "Yes, Sarah's right. We really should be going." She turned to Frederick and offered her hand. "Thank you for your hospitality to sister and I, Mr. Chessher."

Frederick accepted Grace's dainty hand. "Uh, you're…uh, welcome, Miss Winnie."

Sarah didn't say anything for fear she might burst into tears.

Frederick squinted and rubbed his chin.

"Ta-ta!" Grace said as they went out the door.

9

Not a word was spoken all the way from their uncle's office to the hotel. Inside the lobby, Sarah followed Grace into the atrium and sat down.

Grace sat down too. She patted her honey-blonde hair-do before turning her full attention to her sister. "All right, Sarah, let's start with the real reason we came to Galveston."

Sarah couldn't stop the tears from spilling over her cheeks.

Grace handed her a handkerchief.

Sarah explained the whole story in jerky sentences between wiping her eyes. "And that's all of it." She sat back. "I've never been so embarrassed in my life."

"You should be embarrassed, Sarah Jane McKinney. Whatever were you thinking, coming all the way to Galveston, dallying with a man…and at your age!"

"Have you forgotten I'm nearly eighteen years old, sister?" Sarah dipped her chin in consternation. "And it wasn't my sole intention to come here to see Frederick. I came to discuss the cattle drive with Uncle Jeremiah. How was I to know he was out of town?"

"It seems you got sidetracked."

"Nice detective work. Maybe you should apply as a Pinkerton."

A cloud of silence floated between them.

Grace pushed up from her chair. "All right, then, let's just go home." She offered a hand to Sarah.

They walked toward the desk to retrieve their bags.

"Do you think you could possibly not mention this to Mama?" Sarah asked.

"We'll see." Grace frowned as they stepped in line at the hotel desk.

Sarah's attention was drawn to a posted advertisement sign. *Trail Hand For Hire.* The information stated the man had twenty years' experience on the Shawnee and Chisholm trails, then strangely, a blurb stating they wouldn't work in Dickinson County, Kansas. *Serious inquiries come to Pier 15.*

A young porter came out of a back room carrying one tiny bag and one huge suitcase. Grace gave him a tip and thanked him. She turned and smiled. "Are you ready to go?"

Sarah nodded and lifted her small case.

"Sarah, would it be too much trouble for you to carry my suitcase too?"

How long would she be blackmailed by Grace in exchange for her silence? "Of course, sister. I'd be more than happy to." *What have I gotten myself into?* But she didn't have time to worry about that. Before hefting Grace's bag, Sarah ripped the posted advertisement off the wall. "Follow me. There's one more stop I need to make before we leave Galveston."

~*~

The trolley driver tugged the reigns, and the mules came to a stop.

Bags in hand, Sarah and Grace exited.

An early evening fog rolled in, shrouding Pier 15 in a blanket of unnerving gloom.

Grace dropped her bag and took hold of Sarah's arm. "Sister, this place gives me the creepy crawlies."

Sarah shushed her and listened intently to the surrounding sounds. There was an unidentifiable clanging noise. Was it a bell or something hitting one of the many boats moored along the dock? The smells were familiar, a fishiness combined with fuel odors. Seagulls glided above, a random one or two landed on wooden pylons lining the pier. Their mocking laughter made chills run up and down her spine. This place was definitely the seediest Sarah had ever been, and it was nowhere two young women should be.

Grace didn't deserve to go any farther.

Sarah pointed to a decrepit building across the street advertising an egg, bacon and biscuit breakfast. "Why don't you go wait for me in that restaurant. This won't take very long."

"I can't leave you alone here." Grace protested.

"I'll be fine. I'm going to speak to the man who posted this advertisement at the hotel." She held the sign up. "I won't be but a few minutes." She nudged Grace toward the café. "Now go on. Get something to drink."

Grace pulled her long skirt revealing the dark stains covering the hem. "Oh...all right. I really don't want to get my skirt any dirtier." She dropped the fabric and pointed toward the docks. "But if you're not back soon I'll notify the constable."

"I'll be fine...look." Sarah showed Grace the derringer tucked inside her handbag.

Her sister's jaw dropped open.

"Satisfied?" She walked to Pier 15 leaving her stricken sister behind.

Men hauled heavy crates and rolled big barrels off boats tethered to the dock. One of the men wore a flat cap and held a pencil and clipboard. His writing utensils rested on his knee, which was propped on one of the short pylons.

Sarah made her way toward him.

Flat Cap frowned and gave her the once over. "What do you want?" His voice was gruff.

"Y…yes, I'm looking for this man." Sarah showed him the advertisement. "Do you know where I can find him?"

The man stood to his full, enormous height and looked down at the paper. "What do you want with him? He your daddy?"

"Why no. Of course not." She spat the words at him. "Just please answer my question. Is he here or not?"

The man smiled sardonically and raised his voice. "Hey, Reinhardt. Someone here to see you."

One of the men looked in their direction. Older than most of the young men working on the dock, he rubbed his back after he set a heavy crate on the ground.

Sarah twisted her hands together as he walked toward her.

The man looked older than her father had before he'd died. He was also an extremely handsome man. He pulled off his heavy gloves and ran a hand through his hair slicking it away from his face. The gray at his temples and his black mustache made him look all the more distinguished. When he reached Sarah, he put his fists on his belt. "The name's Reinhardt. Who are you?"

It took all the courage she could muster to hold out the notice. The paper shook in her trembling hand. "I'm Sarah McKinney. I saw this advertisement posted at the hotel and I'm interested in hiring you."

"Is that so? You don't look old enough to be away from your mama. And just what would you know about cattle anyway?" He shook his head, threw the paper on the ground, and walked away.

Sarah's spine stiffened. "Look, mister! All you need to know is that I own over a thousand head of cattle and I need to drive them from Bolivar up to High Island. The advertisement said you're an experienced hand, and that's what I'm looking for. Now do you want to come work for me, or do you want to stay here and lift crates, old man?"

Reinhardt turned with a mocking smile. "Them's some mighty strong words coming from such a little ol' girl."

Sarah picked up the paper and pulled a pencil from her reticule. She scribbled on the back then shoved it toward him. "Here's what the job pays. Are you interested or not?"

He looked down at her writing, scratched his chin, and nodded his head. "All right. I'll take it. But let's get one thing straight." He pointed a long, stiff finger at Sarah. "I'm the trail boss."

"Fine…just don't forget. You work for me." She took the flyer, wrote some more, and then handed it to Reinhardt. "Get a crew together as soon as you can. Here's the directions to my place. Mr. Reinhardt…my family is in a bad way right now, and I really need your help. Please don't let me down." Sarah turned to leave.

"What did you say your name was?"

"Sarah McKinney...I..." Sarah replied. "I own the MK Ranch in Bolivar."

"You can count on me, Sarah McKinney."

She gave him a nod before walking away from Pier 15. *Well, he may not be Mr. Frederick Chessher, but he's certainly the man for the job.*

10

There was much work that needed to be done, but Frederick's brain wasn't performing as it should. He reclined in his desk chair and stared at nothing. His mind was feasting on long, blonde tresses, sun-kissed cheeks, and eyes so blue a man could get lost in them. *Oh, how you distract me, Miss McKinney…*

Sarah Jane infiltrated his mind, his heart, his very being. She was so strong and independent with her rugged Texas spirit. She could transform into a sophisticated gentlewoman in the blink of an eye. She was like a wild tiger wrapped inside a delicate rose. *How could such an amazing creature be interested in the likes of me?*

"Are you all right, Mr. Chessher?" Mrs. Gilley stood at the office door. Her entrance snapped Frederick back to reality. "You look as if you're in a trance."

Frederick bolted upright and fumbled with some papers. "Oh, uh, yes, of course I'm all right. I just have a lot on my mind and…and I suppose I'm tired. Yes, that's it, I'm tired." He sat back and rubbed his eyes.

"Here's the Garner file." She shoved it toward him. "It took me forever to find it."

"Whatever are you giving me that for?" Frederick scowled. "That case has been closed for more than a year."

Mrs. Gilley glared back. "That's exactly what I said to you when you asked me to fetch it earlier." She released the heavy ream of legal papers with a thud on Frederick's desk. "And who is this Miss McKinney, and why does she have you in such a frenzy? I could hear your conversation from the other room."

Frederick crossed his arms and looked down. He couldn't stop the burning flush creeping up his neck. "I…"

Mrs. Gilley sucked in an audible gasp, and her eyebrows arched high. "Mr. Chessher! You have feelings for Miss McKinney!"

"Whatever are you talking about?" Frederick shook his head in denial as he fished for a reply. "Certainly, you are mistaken. Miss McKinney happens to be the niece of your boss, and if you had half a mind, you would have treated her and her sister a little more graciously."

The young woman's eyes narrowed. "I don't think I'm mistaken one bit. And to think…you have a precious young lady friend waiting for you in Beaumont. You should be ashamed." Mrs. Gilley charged out of the room.

Thank goodness, that's over. Frederick shuffled through a stack of documents Mr. Logan had asked him to handle. The City of Galveston was thriving, and lawyers were in demand. He was grateful to have a position under one of the best. Frederick looked for the J. L. Rose file. Mr. Logan told him it was a priority. "Rose, Rose, Rose…where are you, Rose?" He froze. His thoughts betrayed him once again. *What's in a name? That which we call a rose, by any other name would smell as sweet.* Shakespeare's words resonated through his mind. *Oh, Sarah…my beautiful rose in fullest of bloom.*

His eyes widened at his shameless desires. *Why is this happening to me?* "Mrs. Gilley! Come to my office at once!"

"What is it?" She came in with a flustered expression.

"I need you to send a telegram right away."

"Let me get pencil and paper." She went out and returned. "Go ahead, I'm ready."

"Eliza, traveling to Beaumont on the weekend. Please be prepared to accept me. Sign it…" Frederick struggled with how to end the message. "Oh, just sign it, sincerely, Frederick."

Mrs. Gilley dipped her chin. She stalked out of his office radiating disapproval.

~*~

Tired of hair slapping her face, Sarah turned into the wind. The ferryboat was slow, but a stiff Gulf breeze was blowing, making it hard to keep her eyes open. She gave up and let them close. Unwanted as they were, thoughts of Frederick came to the forefront of her mind.

His words taunted her. *"I have a lady friend in Beaumont…she would interpret our hand holding as entirely inappropriate."*

Her emotions were all jumbled up. She was mad and confused that he had called her a distraction. Was she not as good as his Beaumont lady? *Oh, Lord, it's my time to start courting. Why is the only man I've ever been interested in already taken? Help me get him out of my mind.* She felt so angry, rejected and…jealous. A tear rolled down her cheek. She swiped it away. *Stupid man…you don't even fear the Lord! You and your stupid emerald-green eyes and your stupid long, brown hair. Why do I even bother trying? And what a stupid name…Frederick Chessher. Sounds like that stupid cat in Alice's Adventures in Wonderland. Oh, Frederick…Fred-er-ick…Freedrick…Freddy…Fritz. Good morning, Fritz…*

"Stop!" Sarah clamped her hand over her mouth.

"Stop what?" Grace swung her head toward her sister.

"Oh, sorry. I'm tired of the wind in my eyes."

"So you thought you would tell it to stop." Grace grinned.

"I know…stupid."

Despite the breeze fluttering its pages, Grace went back to writing in her journal.

Sarah didn't need to be thinking of such things when she had a trail drive to get ready for. Someone would have to travel with her. She wasn't comfortable being alone with Mr. Reinhardt, and Mama wouldn't allow it anyway. She glanced at her sister, contemplating if she could handle the trail drive. Closing her eyes, she chuckled.

Grace grimaced. "Now what's the matter with you?"

"Oh, I'm sorry. I just had a really funny thought go through my mind."

"Would you like to share?"

"No. You wouldn't understand."

"Fine, suit yourself."

Sarah squeezed her small handbag. She smoothed her fingers over the cool metal outline of her pistol. *Mr. Reinhardt, you'd better think twice before messing with me.*

11

"Would you just listen to the noise that rabble is making out back!" Louise let the kitchen curtain fall back in place.

Sarah continued cutting potatoes.

Grace poured cornmeal into a bowl. "Now, Louise, you shouldn't talk about Sarah's hired hands like that." She grinned mischievously at Sarah.

"They aren't my hired hands, Grace. They work for Mr. Reinhardt, who works for me."

Mama turned from the stove. "That Mr. Reinhardt is one handsome man, and rugged too. I've seen him out there working with the cattle. Now that's a cowboy!"

"Ew, Mama, don't talk like that. You're too old to think about men in that way. Besides, Mr. Reinhardt is absolutely revolting," Louise said.

"Have you seen the tobacco spittle running down his chin, and how he scratches himself?" Grace shuddered and picked up an egg.

"I can't believe I raised such prissy girls! The three of you wouldn't know a manly man if you saw one." Mama's tone was lofty.

"Don't include me with those two, Mama. I like manly men." Sarah frowned at her mother.

"Oh? Like who, Sarah? Frederick Chessher?" Grace asked.

"Hold your tongue, Grace!"

"What's this all about?"

"It's nothing, Mama. Grace doesn't know what she's talking about."

Grace wrinkled her nose at Sarah.

"Hush up, you two." Mama had a faraway look in her eyes. "I don't know…having Mr. Reinhardt here reminds me of how virile and handsome Sarah's daddy was. It takes a mighty strong man to run a ranch."

"Yeah, Sarah, Mr. Reinhardt is a good-looking man, and he's proven how much he knows about cattle." Louise patted her belly. "Since you want to run this ranch so bad then maybe you should marry him."

Louise and Grace had a laugh.

Sarah glared at them. "He's an old man, Louise! He might be handsome, but if you knew Reinhardt, you wouldn't even want me going on the cattle drive with him."

Concern washed over Mama's face. "Why do you say that? Has he given you reason to doubt his integrity?"

"You don't need to worry about me, Mama. I'll have Pedro and Inez to protect me. Besides, there are two more things I'm taking to ensure my safety."

"Oh, what's that?"

"My Derringer pistol and Daddy's Winchester rifle." Sarah was convinced she'd be safe on the trail.

~*~

Sarah leaned against a fence post and watched the vaqueros practice their roping skills. The three days they had camped out on the ranch with Reinhardt gave her time to see how proficient the men were with handling cattle.

Reinhardt ambled up beside her and crossed his arms. "Good lookin' bunch of vaqueros, aren't they?"

"I don't know about that, but they sure know what they're doing."

"Yeah, they do…even if they're a bunch of pepper bellies."

"Don't call them that."

"Just calling it the way I see it."

"They *are* a wild bunch. Mama is none too happy about all their singing and carousing until all hours of the night. She's afraid to let me go with you."

"I can appreciate that. I'll see what I can do." Reinhardt rubbed his chin. "So, how's the supply gathering coming?"

"Almost done. We're still on schedule to head out in the morning. How about you, are your men ready?"

"Ready as they'll ever be." Reinhardt stretched and yawned. "That Mexican woman of yours a good cook?"

"Inez happens to be a good cook, as well as close as a family member to us." Sarah didn't contain the censure in her voice.

He held his hands up. "Oh, well, pardon me. I just want to make sure me and my men have some good grub to eat. A man can work up a powerful appetite driving cattle."

"You don't need to worry. Inez will make sure you and your men won't go hungry."

"Mr. Reinhardt…there's something I've been meaning to ask you."

"Oh yeah, what's that?"

"On your advertisement you stated you wouldn't work in Dickinson County, Kansas. Would you mind telling me what that's all about?"

Reinhardt acknowledged her question with a slight nod. "Young lady, you might as well learn now that not everyone in the world is honest and trustworthy like you might think."

Sarah's thoughts turned to one Laird Crosby. In no way did she think everyone was honest or trustworthy. "I don't think that, Mr. Reinhardt."

"Good. Then I'll just say that I worked hard for a man and wasn't paid the money I was promised. So I took something of theirs in exchange for what I was owed. Don't know for sure, but there might be a bounty on my head."

Sarah's eyes grew. "What did you take?"

Reinhardt got a faraway look in his eyes. "She was a tall, beautiful blonde with the longest legs you could ever imagine. And best of all, she didn't even mind going away with me."

A loud gasp escaped Sarah's lips. "Mr. Reinhardt!"

The man laughed loudly as he walked toward the stock pens. He put two fingers in his mouth and whistled three sharp notes.

When the magnificent Palomino trotted toward him, Sarah's shoulders dropped, frustrated. *Oh, how ignorant can I be! Beautiful, tall, blonde…horse!*

12

The streets of downtown Beaumont, Texas bustled with activity. Lumber for the railroad was in great demand, and a seemingly endless supply floated down the Neches River daily. Towering mansions surrounding the outskirts of the city reeked of wealth. Lumber and rice barons owned the town, and Eliza Broussard's father was one of them.

Frederick stepped out of the cab and paid the driver. Five steps led up to the front door of the town house where the Broussards stayed when not at their country estate. Frederick rang the bell and waited.

After a few moments a plump little housekeeper opened the door. Her uniform was starched and pressed to perfection. Upon seeing Frederick, her cheeks rounded to tiny brown apples. "Mr. Chessher." She stepped back allowing him entrance.

"Hello, Rachel."

"I was wondering when you was going to be here. The train running late?"

Frederick began shrugging off his overcoat. She helped ease it off his shoulders and folded it over her arm.

"Uh, yes, there was a slight delay. A few stray cattle blocked the tracks."

Rachel shook her head. "Oh, my heavens. Them cows sure can be a problem."

"Yes, I suppose you're right about that."

"I'd rather they be on a dinner plate than the railroad track." Rachel laughed at her joke.

Frederick smiled halfheartedly.

Rachel narrowed her eyes. "You all right, Mr. Chessher? Can I get you something to drink, maybe some tea, or a cool glass of lemonade?"

"Oh, no thank you, Rachel. Please inform Miss Broussard of my arrival."

"Yes sir, Mr. Chessher. I'll let her know directly. You can wait in the parlor." She gestured toward the seating area, his coat still draped over her arm. Then she toddled up the lavish marble staircase at a fast clip.

Frederick walked to the parlor. He sat next to a large picture window looking out onto the street. Gazing at the passersby, Frederick mentally checked off the tasks he needed to do at the law firm. Had he neglected anything Mr. Logan had asked of him? He certainly hoped not, but having left town so quickly he wasn't sure.

A woman passed in front of the window holding onto the arm of a tall man with brownish colored hair. Blonde curls flowed out from beneath her wide-brimmed hat. He shook his head to remove the uninvited image of another head of blonde curls from his mind. But it was useless; her face was permanently emblazoned there.

Frederick drummed his fingers on the arm of his chair. He then pulled his watch from his waistcoat and looked at the time. An unwelcome wariness overcame him, and his guard came up. Why did Eliza see fit to keep him waiting at his every visit? Was his time not as important as hers? He hammered the armchair with his fist. *Who does she think she is making me wait like this? I have an important position, and deserve better than to be treated this way.* "Well…that's it." Frederick stood to leave.

Eliza entered the room. "Frederick, darling, I see you've arrived safely. Your message took me by surprise. I wasn't expecting you for another week." Eliza stopped halfway down the stairs.

Her southern drawl didn't charm Frederick as it once had. In fact, it sounded fake. And she would not apologize for making him wait. He met her and offered his elbow. "Eliza."

"Thank you, Frederick." Eliza linked arms and sashayed down the stairs. "Even though your visit is unexpected I'm glad you're here. This gives us more time to discuss our plans."

Frederick escorted Eliza to a table with two chairs in the parlor. "Our plans?" He questioned.

"Why yes, you silly man. Our engagement plans, of course."

"Oh?" While Frederick wasn't surprised at Eliza's boldness, he was astounded at this presumption. He took a seat in the other chair.

"Rachel!" Eliza hollered toward the door. "Come into the parlor at once!"

Frederick startled.

Rachel rushed through the door to Eliza's side. "Yes, ma'am?"

"Rachel…fetch a pitcher of lemonade and two glasses for Mr. Chessher and myself." Eliza spoke to the woman in a contemptuous tone.

Frederick looked at this woman, the one he'd considered marrying. Then he glanced at Rachel. He'd never met a housekeeper with a sweeter disposition. Why did Eliza treat her with such disrespect? And why had he never noticed this about Eliza before? He crushed thoughts of Sarah and her kindness to everyone.

"Yes, ma'am, Miss Eliza. I'll bring it right away."

"See that you do."

Rachel scurried out of the room.

Had he been so infatuated with Eliza that he never realized how rude and demanding she was with the servants?

"Now back to our conversation. Whenever you do finally get up the nerve to ask me to marry you, I already have everything planned. Our engagement party will be the event of the season." Eliza picked up a small candy dish from the table and took a sweet treat for herself. "Candy?" She offered the bowl to Frederick.

"No thank you."

"Oh, Frederick, Delia and I have been shopping for everything a new bride could possibly need."

"Delia, your girlfriend from school?"

"Yes, of course, silly." She grimaced at him. "Honestly, Frederick, what other Delia do we know?"

Frederick overlooked the condescending tone she used with him.

Rachel hurried through the doorway. She held a large silver tray with a pitcher of lemonade, two glasses and a dish of delicious looking cakes. "Here you are, Miss Eliza, some nice, fresh lemonade, and cakes." Rachel sat the tray on the table and picked up a glass and the pitcher. She began pouring the lemonade as Eliza's poodle ran into the parlor barking viciously at Frederick. Startled by the intrusion, Rachel spilled lemonade on herself, the silver platter, and her employer.

Eliza shrieked and flailed her arms about, showering Frederick and the poodle with drops of lemonade.

Rachel removed a small towel from her apron and dabbed at the liquid on Eliza's arms.

"Look what you've done, you...you idiot!" Eliza screamed at Rachel. "And stop touching me with that filthy rag. Go get a clean towel."

"I'm so sorry, Miss Eliza!" Rachel ran from the room.

Eliza continued holding her arms away from her body. The little poodle dog sneezed and then shook, sending lemonade flying from his fur.

Frederick removed his glasses and wiped the sticky liquid from his face.

"Oh, my poor Penny Poo. Did that bad woman get lemonade on you, my precious?"

"It wasn't her fault, Eliza. If your dog didn't despise me this might not have happened."

Eliza glared at Frederick. "It looks like she got you too."

"I think this might have come from dear Penny Poo."

Rachel rushed into the parlor with three fresh towels. She handed one to Eliza, and one to Frederick before kneeling to wipe Penny's fur.

"That will be all, Rachel...thank you," Eliza said begrudgingly.

Rachel stood and nodded her acknowledgement.

The poodle commenced with her verbal attack on Frederick.

"Rachel, please take Penny with you on your way out."

"Yes, ma'am." Rachel scooped up the barking

menace and left the parlor.

"Now then, what were we talking about before all the commotion started? Oh, yes, I was telling you about Delia and the engagement party we've been planning. If *someone* would stop wasting time and ask me to marry them, that is."

Frederick crossed his legs and folded his hands. "Yes, you definitely need an engagement in order to have an engagement party."

"Oh, Frederick it will be so wonderful. The party's theme is Paris, France! Doesn't that sound marvelous?"

"Oui, oui."

Eliza didn't acknowledge the terse sarcasm in his answer or look at him as she gushed about the party she was planning.

And suddenly Frederick realized he had never been an integral part of their relationship. His role was Eliza's silent partner.

"And we won't have to worry about a thing. Papa will pay for everything…when you ask me, of course."

At some point Frederick stopped listening to Eliza prattle on. His mind had traveled a great distance away, to a rustic ranch house on a quiet peninsula to the west of Beaumont.

"I've been thinking about our honeymoon too! Delia says we should go somewhere exotic. Wouldn't that be a wonderful way to begin our romance?"

Romance…sunbeams shine down on the front porch. Cattle are lowing softly in the distance. The door slowly opens.

"And after we return from our honeymoon we can buy that house that's for sale down the way from Mama and Papa. Mama said Papa has already inquired about it for us!"

Then she steps out onto the porch. She turns her head at the sound of a horse's soft nickering. Her natural beauty is illuminated in the evening light.

"Oh, and best of all, I spoke to Papa, and he has made arrangements for you to sign on at the law office he uses right here in town. You are going to be Papa's personal attorney!"

A brisk sea breeze blows. Her long, golden tresses float around her porcelain face. She twirls around to face the wind. Her flowing green skirt dances in the breeze.

"Isn't this all so exciting, Frederick?"

She breathes deeply, and brushes blonde locks away from her face.

"Frederick! Are you listening to me?"

Frederick blinked and snapped his gaze toward Eliza. "What, what? Yes, I'm listening to you."

"You haven't heard a single word I've said."

"Of course I have. You were talking about all the plans you and Delia have made." Frederick pasted on a smile.

Eliza's eyes grew wide, and her lips thinned to a tight line. She rose from her chair and stared at Frederick before huffing out a breath. Without a word, she stomped toward the door.

"Eliza, wait, don't leave!"

But she was gone.

13

"Can't you make them stop?" Sarah hollered her question to Reinhardt in order to be heard over the vaqueros.

"Aw, they're just excited. A little hootin' and hollerin' ain't gonna hurt no one."

Sarah scowled and pointed to the cattle, restless and bawling. "They're upsetting the herd."

"All right, all right." Reinhardt chuckled, sauntering off on bowed legs.

Mama motioned for Sarah to approach. "Sarah, honey, I need to talk to you before you leave."

Sarah was eager to get the herd moving.

Mama stepped away from the rest of the family who had gathered to see the riders off. "Now if any of those men are mean to you, or if you get scared one little bit, you tell Pedro and Inez. They will protect you."

"I'm not scared, Mama. And I don't need anyone to protect me. I've got Rex, and I've got Daddy's rifle, loaded and strapped to my saddle." She put her hand down and scratched Rex's head. "Besides, they better not mess with me if they want to get paid at the end of the drive."

The family gathered in a circle, and Guy Claiborne led them in a prayer for safety. They said their goodbyes and waved while Sarah climbed onto Ginger's saddle. The horse whinnied with eagerness.

Sarah raised her hand, anxious to give the call to head out.

"Let's ride!" Reinhardt bellowed loudly dampening Sarah's small voice.

Rex barked wildly.

The vaqueros yipped and yelped, calling out to the herd.

The cattle bawled as they slowly lumbered toward the road.

Sarah's anger rose. Reinhardt had spoiled her plan to take charge.

Reinhardt glanced over at her. "What'cha waitin' for little girl? Yer mommy ain't coming with us."

She glared and snapped Ginger's reigns. "Ya!" The horse bucked and took off like a shot. Sarah was happy she'd left Reinhardt behind, but it infuriated her when she heard him laughing.

~*~

Ginger settled into a steady trot with Rex walking close to Ginger.

Sarah stayed nearby the vaquero who rode flank. It was the best place to keep an eye on everything without Reinhardt watching her every move.

She'd had men treat her much the same way when she was a girl, learning at her father's side. But that was different; Daddy was the boss then. She was the boss now. But for some reason she couldn't shake the feeling she'd fallen into some horrible trap devised by Reinhardt and his men. And she would never forgive herself if Pedro and Inez fell victim too.

The longhorn cattle took little time falling into a sturdy forward pace. More than four hundred years of breeding produced a gentle natured animal with a strong resolve, capable of surviving the harshest of conditions.

Pedro and Inez bumped along the rough terrain in the makeshift chuck wagon they'd pulled together for the trip. Their stubborn donkey kept up with the herd. Inez cuddled close to Pedro's side. How could they be so old and still act like young lovers? That was the kind of relationship she desired…one based on love and trust.

A familiar face invaded Sarah's thoughts. She closed her eyes, attempting to ward it off…to no avail. He wouldn't leave. And in all honesty, she didn't want him to. *Why did I have to go and make a fool of myself, batting my eyes at Frederick?* Sarah tightened her jaw against the tears that threatened. *I was going to teach him to be a rancher. But no, he already has a sophisticated girlfriend. He probably thinks I'm some kind of bumpkin, trying to snag a rich man. Well, the joke's on you, Frederick Chessher. I don't need you or any other man. I can take care of myself just fine!*

"Alto!"

Sarah jolted at Reinhardt's command to stop coming from behind her.

He guffawed.

"You're not as funny as you think you are," Sarah yelled.

"I don't know. My men sure got a kick out of it."

The vaqueros were indeed laughing.

The man's silly antics helped quell Sarah's uneasiness that he had bad intentions in mind. Why else would he go to the trouble of teasing her?

"Why are we stopping anyway? We couldn't have gone more than ten miles."

Reinhardt pulled back on his horse's reins. "I'm stopping for you. Looks like you could use your beauty sleep."

"I think what you're trying to say is that you're too old, and it's past your bedtime. We can push the cattle at least five more miles."

Reinhardt frowned. "We've gone far enough for the day. Because of your family we got a late start. All their huggin' and prayin'." He snorted and shook his head.

"You should try praying sometime. It just might help you."

"It sure ain't helped me this far."

Sarah rode toward Pedro and Inez to tell them what was happening. She would never admit it, but she was exhausted and happy to stop for the day. *I wonder what Reinhardt meant when he said prayer hadn't helped him?*

14

Sarah made sure Rex stayed close by and that the derringer was strapped to her leg while she brushed Ginger's fur. She had two lines of defense while her back was turned on the vaqueros.

The Mexican men had spent the past hour drinking from a brown crockery jug and smoking cigars. Despite slurred speech, they were singing loud and off-key.

Reinhardt hadn't joined them.

The aroma of pinto beans wafted through the campsite. Inez stirred the pot while Pedro flattened balls of tortilla dough. Inez flopped them into a frying pan greased with lard.

Sarah turned her attention to Rex. He looked up at her, his eyes full of puppy love, panting after the long day of work. "Come on, Rex." His tail wagged at the sound of his name. "Let's go get some water and something to eat." The dog barked his approval.

Reinhardt hovered around the food, snatching tortillas when Inez wasn't looking.

"Ouch!" Reinhardt yanked his hand back.

The spry little Mexican woman rattled off a string of Spanish words.

"All right, all right. You can keep yer dern tortillas." Reinhardt rubbed his hand where Inez's spoon had left a mark.

"That'll teach you to mess with Inez." Sarah

laughed.

Reinhardt sat on a downed tree.

Sarah joined him. "I'm surprised to see you're not whooping it up with your men."

"Nah, I'm getting too old for that business. Liquor makes you forget what you done the night before and regret how you feel the morning after."

"Well, I'm glad. Those vaqueros are obnoxious. And they better keep their guns holstered or we might have a stampede on our hands."

"Aw, surely they're not that stupid." Reinhardt picked up a thin piece of wood from the sand and stuck it between his teeth before giving Sarah a goofy smile. "I saw you riding flank with Ramon earlier today. Is he the kind of man you like to kiss?"

"Please! I'd rather kiss a horse's rear end!"

"Well, that can be arranged too." He chuckled. "Maybe I'll tell Ramon you're sweet on him. Then you can kiss him…after you finish brushing my horse, of course."

"You will do no such thing. And I won't be brushing your horse either. Remember, I'm *your* boss— not the other way around." Sarah was beginning to realize that poking fun was Reinhardt's way of showing that he liked her.

"Ven a comer!" Inez gave the call for dinner.

The vaqueros came as fast as they could.

Sarah waited for the vaqueros to clear out before getting up.

Inez handed her a plate of beans and Pedro added a couple tortillas to her dish.

"Gracias, Inez y Pedro."

"De nada, mi hija."

Sarah sat on the tree where she and Reinhardt had

sat before. She bowed her head and thanked God for the food and for keeping them safe. Reinhardt's curious stare unsettled her.

He averted his gaze. Uncertainty shown on his face, and his lips parted. He begrudgingly formed one word to say to Inez. "Gracias."

Sarah turned away so Reinhardt wouldn't see her grin.

~*~

Her bedroll was soft, but the ground was hard, and the wind had died down, making it warmer than usual. Rex lay close by Sarah's side, keeping watch. Not the peaceful night, or the soft Gulf breeze, or the gentle lowing cattle, or even sheer exhaustion could lure Sarah to sleep. She gazed at the stars.

There were plenty of stars, enough for everybody to have one…like men. God provided a man for each of her sisters. Mama had gone through three. Sarah only wanted one, Frederick Chessher. *Why God? If I can't have him, then why did You let him come into my life in the first place? So I could fall for him…like a fool?* Sarah squeezed her eyes shut. She had to turn her thoughts away from Frederick. Her mind wandered to Reinhardt. She shuddered, and then drifted off to sleep in mere moments.

The moon was high in the sky when the cattle, bawling and restless, awakened Sarah. Rex whined and pawed her leg.

"What is it, boy?"

Pedro appeared before her haloed in a ring of lantern light. "Miss Sarah, Miss Sarah, you need to get up." He crouched down beside her feet. "Mr.

Reinhardt say something happen with one of the cows."

Sarah looked in the shadows, found her rifle and headed toward the commotion.

A shot pierced the quiet night.

She ran the rest of the way to the lighted area. The barrel of Reinhardt's pistol smoldered in the cool night air. One of Daddy's cows lay writhing on the ground.

Sarah struggled to form the words she wanted to say. "W…what happened? Why would you shoot my cow?"

Reinhardt pointed his pistol downward. "I didn't. Snake got yer cow."

The huge reptile's head was gone.

Tears swelled and Sarah almost gagged, but she was the boss, and the boss wasn't allowed to cry.

Reinhardt kicked some dirt toward the snake. "It ain't gonna live. Got her in the nose too. Poor old cow was probably curious and bent over to check it out."

Daddy's beautiful longhorn writhed in pain as the poison spread through her body. Sarah wanted to cry along with her.

"She won't make it, Sarah. A bite on the face from a snake that big…she'll swell up and won't be able to breathe. Might as well take care of it now and not let her suffer. You want me to do it?"

"No. I'm responsible for this herd. I'll do it." Sarah raised the rifle hoping Reinhardt wouldn't notice her trembling arms. She pointed Daddy's gun at the cow's head and pulled the trigger. The heart wrenching bawling stopped, and the animal's body went limp.

Reinhardt called his men over and gave them orders in Spanish.

Sarah walked into the darkness. Rex trailed close

behind her. When she reached her bedroll, she put the rifle away and crawled inside the blanket. Rex circled before curling up by her side. She put her arm around Rex and quietly released the flood of tears she'd worked so hard holding in. She didn't cry because she shot *a* cow, but because she'd shot Daddy's cow. She'd failed him. *Oh, Lord, why did You take my daddy away from me? Maybe if he'd been here none of this would be happening. I don't have a daddy. I don't have a boyfriend. And I'm not strong enough to do this without someone to help me!*

The anger rising inside gave her comfort. It gave her power. Was Daddy giving her the strength to finish? No…Daddy was gone, and Frederick was not hers. But there was One who gave her comfort, One who gave her strength, One who would never ever leave her.

15

"Mrs. Logan, please, I couldn't possibly eat another bite." Frederick held his hands up to the tiny woman. She didn't seem to take him seriously. Could he risk refusing his boss's wife's food?

"Bitte essen!" She pleaded, pushing strands of salt and ginger hair back into her tight bun.

"Wilma, stop begging the boy to eat. He clearly doesn't want any more food."

"Sie sind zu dünn."

Jeremiah Logan smiled at his little German wife before turning to Frederick. "She says you're too skinny."

Frederick chuckled and put his hand on his stomach. "I won't be if I stay here much longer."

Mr. Logan placed his hand against his wife's back. Her laugh lines smoothed away when she smiled at him. Their love for one another was evident by the simple looks they shared. It was real, it was alive, it was the kind of relationship Frederick desired to have. But he never would, not with Eliza Broussard.

Mrs. Logan turned away and continued heaping food onto Frederick's plate.

"You might as well give up, Frederick. Take the food. She'll wrap it up for you to take home. It's what she does. She cooks. How do you think I got this?" He patted his round belly. "Besides, you need to leave room for dessert…apple strudel."

Frederick put his palms on the table. "Oh, no, no, please, I couldn't possibly eat dessert."

A thunder of feet approached the dining room door. Their five grandchildren trooped into the room.

The oldest, no more than six or seven years old, ran to his grandfather's side. "Papa, Papa, can we have apple strudel?"

A girl with golden-blonde ringlets pleaded. "Peas, peas, peas, can we have strudels, Papa?"

Mr. Logan pulled the little girl onto his lap and laughed. "Of course you can, Jess."

She hugged his neck.

The remaining three children, not old enough to form sentences, gathered around his knees.

The little girl with the blonde curls looked a lot like her gorgeous older cousin…Sarah.

Mrs. Logan herded the children like a mother hen gathering her chicks. "*Komm, komm.* Here we go."

They moved to the living room amidst cries for their papa, and of course, strudel.

Mr. Logan smiled as they left the room.

"You are a lucky man, Mr. Logan. A wonderful wife, five beautiful grandkids." Frederick lifted his hands to his surroundings. "Not to mention this handsome island villa."

"And don't forget my ranch in Houston." The older man teased and chuckled. "These are my daughter's children. They're visiting from Dallas. I love them to death, but I'm glad they're going home in a few days. We have seven more…three in Houston and four in Mississippi. But you are right. Only Wilma and I don't say we are lucky. We say that we are blessed. God has richly blessed my family."

Frederick believed there was a God, but he

couldn't say that he knew much about Him. Sarah sure seemed to care about such things. Would the fact that he wasn't a religious man stand in the way of him having a relationship with her? *Oh, my word…what am I thinking? I'm already in a relationship with…with…* Frederick wracked his brain to remember her name. *Eliza!* He shook his head in disbelief.

Mr. Logan stood and patted Frederick on the shoulder. "Let's go out on the veranda. You look as if you could use some fresh air."

A pleasant breeze blew in from the Gulf.

Mr. Logan sat in a black iron chair. He opened an inlaid wood box sitting on the round iron table between them, and then handed a fat cigar to Frederick. He clipped the end off his cigar before giving the cutter to Frederick. He sat back and released a cloud of smoke into the air.

Frederick struck a match and did the same, only he coughed for a minute.

"Nothing like a good cigar after a satisfying meal." The older man raised his legs and rested them on one of the chairs.

"I agree wholeheartedly." A soft, steady breeze flipped Frederick's hair about.

"Um-hm. So tell me, what do you think President McKinley's next move will be in the Philippines?"

"It's hard to say, but I read that our boys suffered heavy casualties in the most recent skirmish on Mindanao. He can't be too happy about that."

"No, I wouldn't think so. Makes him look bad, and that's not good when he's up for re-election in November!" Mr. Logan puffed on his cigar. "Say, did you get that land deal taken care of for Bettencourt? He came by asking about it."

"Yes, I did. In fact, the papers were sent to him today."

"Good, good. I like to keep him happy. A lot of money there. And he's a good man too. There's a lot to be said about a man with money, and of good character too."

"Yes, I haven't forgotten what you said about making sure our clients are always happy. And I've taken it upon myself to make certain Mr. Bettencourt is personally taken care of." Mr. Logan discerning eyes made him anxious. He nervously tapped the ash from his cigar.

"Speaking of men with a lot of money, I spoke to Mr. Broussard the other day. Seems his office received one of the first telephone lines."

Frederick tugged at his collar. Apprehension flowed through him. "Oh…is that right?"

"Yes, said I was his very first call. Wanted to talk about the visit you made."

"You mean to tell me that he is fortunate enough to have received the very first telephone line in the whole town, and he called you to talk about…me?"

"That's right."

Heat crept up his neck. "I didn't even see Mr. Broussard on my visit. Whatever did he want to discuss concerning me?"

Mr. Logan dusted the ashes from his cigar. "Mr. Broussard told me that according to his daughter, Eliza, there seems to be trouble in paradise. Is that true?"

Frederick dropped back into the chair. "If you mean that I'm not comfortable with being told when I should propose, where I shall live, and with whom I shall work, then yes, there might be a bit of trouble!"

His irritated stated caused him to stammer. "She…she…Eliza Broussard is an absolutely shameless woman, sir."

Mr. Logan chuckled. "Sounds like you have some woman troubles on your hands, son. So tell me, why haven't you asked her to marry you yet?"

Frederick sighed while he snubbed out his cigar in the ashtray. "I…I don't know how to answer that question, sir."

"What is it? Is she ugly?"

"Mr. Logan…"

"Well, I don't know. I've never met the girl." The man laughed.

"I guess I just…I suppose…I don't love her, sir."

"That can be a problem." He twirled his cigar. "Her father is chomping at the bit for you to pop the question. What are you going to do about it?"

That's an excellent question? What am I going to do about it? He folded his arms and looked his boss in the eye. "I can honestly tell you that I have absolutely no idea."

Mr. Logan pointed with his cigar. "You know, Frederick, I've been hearing a lot of rumors about you lately."

"Go on."

"I understand that while I was out of town you had a couple visitors from across the peninsula."

He would have to speak to the office help about what was inappropriate to discuss with their boss. "Uh, um yes, that's right. It seems that two of your nieces came to see you. You'll be happy to know that I treated them, well, at least one of them, to lunch. Unfortunately, I took them to the German diner."

"Nothing wrong with that."

"No, except that it was kraut and bratwurst day."

Mr. Logan's lips puckered. "Oh, pungent, huh?"

"Yes, I'm afraid so."

"It was revealed to me by Mrs. Gilley that perhaps my youngest niece might have had an ulterior motive than why she claimed to be in Galveston."

Frederick remained tight lipped.

"I wouldn't have believed it coming from anyone else, but I've learned over the years that my secretary is a mighty trustworthy source of information. With that being said, she also mentioned that you seem to have your own *ulterior motives* in regards to my niece."

Frederick was afraid to speak.

The large man leaned forward, and their light conversation suddenly turned to sobering discourse. He pointed at Frederick with the butt of his cigar. "Now you listen here, boy. It sounds to me like you're in way over your head. I don't know Miss Broussard from Adam, but Sarah Jane is family…my family. And if you think for one minute that you'll have a relationship with Eliza Broussard, and one on the side with my Sarah, then you've got another think coming."

"No, sir! I would never do that, especially not to Sarah."

Mr. Logan relaxed.

"Sir, I don't know what's come over me. I thought I knew exactly what I wanted in life. Eliza and I were going to be married, and…but everything changed when I met your niece. Now I know that I don't love Eliza." Frederick rubbed his temples. "I'm not sure I even like her anymore."

Mr. Logan leaned back and put his feet back up on the chair. "Thank you, son. I didn't take you for that kind of man. Now I'm counting on you to do the right thing, whatever that may be, in regards to both Eliza and Sarah. But I have some sage advice I'll share with you. Don't ever ask a woman to marry you if you don't love her." The older man extended his hand.

Frederick grasped it firmly. "Thank you, sir. I won't let you down. I promise."

Mr. Logan laughed, continuing to hold Frederick's hand. "I know you won't. Your job depends on it."

Frederick laughed too.

"All right, then. You ready for some apple strudel?"

"I suppose I'm as ready as I'll ever be."

Both men stood and headed for the door.

Mr. Logan rapped him hard on the back. "Wilma was right. We do need to put some meat on your bones, son!"

16

Morning dawned bright on the second day of the drive.

The cattle were scattered, but the vaqueros were in no shape to reign in the herd. The previous night of drinking and carousing left them worse for wear.

Sarah leaned back against the chuck wagon. She swirled her biscuit in a plate of gravy and took a bite. The hired hands had drunk almost all the coffee. Salt pork stuck in her throat, and there was nothing to wash it down with, so she tossed it.

Rex greedily snatched it out of the air and swallowed it down.

She dunked her plate into the washtub by Inez's work table.

"Gracias, Missy Sarah."

Sarah smiled. *No sense sitting around wasting time.* "Saddle up!"

Her command was met with moaning and groaning from the three vaqueros, followed by a slur of words that made Sarah glad she wasn't fluent in Spanish. Though they didn't mind cursing her, they didn't do what she said either. And she was fairly sure they understood what she wanted.

Pedro said something to Inez. A heated Spanish debate broke out. Inez scowled at Pedro, harrumphed, then went back to her work.

"Is everything all right, Pedro?"

He shoved his hands into his trouser pockets. "She say she need to stay here. She need more time to cut up that cow into steaks."

"Oh, all right." It took Sarah a few seconds to realize he was referring to the cow she'd shot the night before.

"She say she have tortillas and cheese cut up for the men to eat. But she not ready to go yet."

"That's fine. You stay here and help her. I'm sure it won't be any trouble for you to catch up with us before nightfall."

"Thank you, Miss Sarah."

The vaqueros hadn't moved.

"Saddle up! We're leaving!" She turned to Reinhardt. "Why won't they do anything I say? Did you tell them not to listen to me?"

"Now why would I do something like that?" He grinned, making Sarah fume all the more. "All right, now. Don't get all red in the face."

Reinhardt groaned and got up. After taking his plate over to the washtub, he cupped his hands and hollered at the vaqueros. "Vamos!"

The three men jumped up. Within minutes they were saddled, and the cattle drive was underway once again. The look of pity on Reinhardt's face was maddening.

~*~

Driving the cattle across the Bolivar Peninsula was slow.

Who would have thought so many changes would happen in such a short period of time? Daddy hadn't been gone all that long, and already Sarah was moving on with her life. Ranching was Daddy's business. He'd loved it. He'd taught Sarah to love it too. And as soon as she sold the herd off in High Island, she would have plenty of money to do as she pleased, wherever she pleased. She had to ship Daddy's breed stock to Uncle Jeremiah's ranch in Houston. Then she needed to find a ranch of her own, since Mama wanted to turn her place into a boarding house. Maybe Sarah could find a spread close to her aunt and uncle. She might even run into Frederick if he should visit Uncle Jeremiah. Defeat beckoned. *Oh, Lord, how can I do this when people look at me like I'm just a kid? I have McKinney blood running through my veins, and McKinney's are a strong breed, just like our cattle.* She sniffed and wiped her eyes. Her own frailty and self-pity embarrassed her.

One of the cows bawled in obvious pain. A huge, pregnant cow fell on her side.

"Reinhardt, hold up!"

He didn't hear her.

She put fingers to her lips and let out a deafening whistle.

All four men turned.

She raised her arms, palms toward them. "Stop!"

Reinhardt raised his right arm making a fist. "Alto!" He called out to the vaqueros, and rode toward Sarah.

"We have a pregnant cow down. I thought we had more time." She yelled over the din of mooing cows and Rex's loud barking.

"Com'on." He said, whipping the rains of his horse.

Reaching the downed animal, they dismounted and knelt beside her.

"I was afraid this might happen. She was lookin' a

little iffy this morning."

"Then why didn't you say something?" Sarah asked.

Reinhardt grimaced. "Ain't nothin' we could'a done anyway. Calf's gonna come when it gets good and ready." He picked up the cow's tail and took a closer look. "Yep, won't be long now. We're gonna have to stop here for the day."

"We can't stop here…we need to get to the other side of Rollover Pass!"

"Well, looks as if your cow has different plans because her calf is coming now."

Sarah groaned. Rollover Pass was a dangerous crossing if the timing wasn't right. And this delay could be the thing that put them in the middle of a very bad situation.

The cow bawled out, and her calf was born.

Sarah rubbed the exhausted cow's side. "Come on, girl. You need to get up and take care of your baby."

The little calf wiggled around, snorting to clear its nose and trying to rise.

Rex pawed the baby and growled at her.

Reinhardt scratched his chin and then lifted the cow's tail again. "Yeah, I thought so."

"What is it?"

"She ain't done yet, that's what."

"Twins?"

"Yep."

"She's having trouble."

"Yeah, she's all tired out. We'll give her a little time. If she still ain't calved, I'll pull it."

The first calf was a strong little heifer. In no time at all, she was up and bawling her complaints.

Sarah took a piece of feedbag cloth from her

saddlebag and rubbed the calf down.

Each time the little heifer bawled the mama cow cried along with her. This seemed to help progress the birthing of the second calf.

"Well, look at that. The calf's coming on its own."

A few minutes later the cow gave one final cry and pushed out her second calf. Then she rolled over and got up. The first calf bawled for her mama, but her sister didn't move.

"She's not breathing." Sarah swatted the calf on the rear end, but still, no movement. "Come on girl, wake up." In a last-ditch effort, Sarah picked up a piece of straw and swabbed it inside the calf's nose. Nothing. She tried again, only this time she poked at the inside of her nose. The calf sneezed, and bloody snot flew everywhere.

The mama cow came to her calf and nudged her with her snout. The smaller twin calf got up on her feet at her mother's urging, bawling all the while.

Sarah wiped her brow on her shirtsleeve. "Whew, didn't think she was going to make it.".

"Well, we lost one cow, but added two more."

Another cow cried out from the herd.

Reinhardt pushed his hat back on his head. "There goes another one. I thought we had more time with her."

"Dang it, Brutus!" Sarah cursed her father's prize bull.

The second cow gave birth with no need to intervene.

"You did a good job back there." Reinhardt spoke without looking her in the eye.

"What do you mean?"

"How you worked with that calf until she started

breathing on her own. She might have died otherwise."

Sarah's cheeks warmed. "Just doing what I had to do."

"Um-hm." He walked away.

As the sun began its slow descent into the West, the newborn calves romped and played. A trail of dust kicked up behind Pedro and Inez approaching in the wagon.

The vaqueros cheered.

The cooks worked quickly, unloading dishes and the delicious smelling food.

In short order the vaqueros were in a line waiting to be served a heaping bowl of pinto beans. Each one of the vaqueros thanked Inez when she handed them their meal.

Sarah accepted her food and thanked the cook.

She joined Reinhardt next to the fire Pedro made and sat down, bowing her head

Reinhardt stood. "All right, everyone, we have a lot to be thankful for, what with three calves being born healthy and all. And we got these good eats too. It only seems right that we should thank God."

Reinhardt was going to pray?

He looked at her. "Go on now, start praying."

"Oh." Sarah was caught off guard, but she worded a prayer of thanksgiving. Later, Sarah laid in her bedroll gazing at the stars. *Thank You, Father, for allowing me to witness the miracle of those baby calves coming into the world, and for letting me be a part of it. Lord, I suppose You know what's come over Reinhardt, even if I don't. But I gotta admit, I sure do like the change.*

17

"Let's go! Let's go!" The vaqueros moved slow, and all of Sarah's coaxing did nothing to speed them up. "Ugh!"

She scanned the herd, hoping and praying nothing would delay them today. They should already be on the other side of Rollover Pass. The tide would be coming in strong all day long. Why didn't anyone listen to her? They didn't understand how important it was to get the cattle across the pass.

A twinge of hope filled Sarah's heart when she saw one of Reinhardt's men running.

But he was running from another vaquero chasing him with a knife and screaming in Spanish.

Oh, Lord, why is this happening to me? Five more miles, that's all I ask, Lord. Five more miles and we'll be at the pass.

Reinhardt took off after the two wayward vaqueros, hollering. He pulled his lariat from his belt and began slinging it in a circle above his head. The looped rope flew through the air before coming down around the arms of the knife wielding man. With one mighty pull, Reinhardt brought the man to the ground. He gathered the slack rope and punched the vaquero in the jaw before removing the knife from his hand.

A string of Spanish words came from Reinhardt's mouth, none of which Sarah understood, which was probably a good thing.

The other vaquero had put some distance between himself and the knife. The third vaquero was laughing so hard that coffee sloshed from his mug onto his britches.

Pedro appeared by Sarah's side.

"Do you know what's going on?"

"Sí, Sí." Pedro pointed toward the man who had been chased. "This man, he tell the other man that his sister is, is, how do you say, much beautiful. He also say that he want to..." Pedro's tan cheeks blushed a shade of red. "He say he want to...I rather not tell you what he say, Miss Sarah."

"I think I understand." *Five more miles, Lord, just five more miles.*

Reinhardt stood over the downed vaquero, and gathered up the loops of rope. The younger man rubbed his jaw. Reinhardt glanced at Sarah, silently assuring her that he had things under control.

"Can we get going now? We *have* to hurry. The tide will be coming in strong all day, and we need to get the herd to the other side of the pass."

"You know, you worry too much."

"Look, you don't have any idea what lies ahead. Have you ever had to cross Rollover Pass?"

"Nope. Never heard of it."

"Exactly. If we had crossed over yesterday, everything would be fine, but with the tide rising it's a whole different story."

"What kind of woman keeps watch on the tides?" Reinhardt mumbled the words under his breath.

"Someone who was born and raised on this peninsula, that's who!"

He shook his head and hollered at his men. *"Vamos, hombres!"*

~*~

"H'ya, h'ya!" Sarah tried to push the cattle faster. It was dangerous moving the herd at high tide. Even the mighty longhorns were no match for the water rushing in from the Gulf of Mexico through Rollover Pass into Galveston Bay.

Reinhardt rode up. "So tell me, what is this pass you're so dern worried about?"

"It's a wallowed-out place in the middle of the road where water passes through from the Gulf to the bay. It's called Rollover Pass because way back when, pirates would roll big barrels full of booty over, instead of taking them into Galveston where they would have to pay customs on it."

"Sounds like a good idea to me."

"Well, you would, wouldn't you?" Sarah snapped back at him.

He laughed.

Sarah couldn't help but laugh along with him. Their light-hearted exchange gave Sarah the courage she needed to ask a question she'd been mulling over. "Say, Reinhardt, you mind me asking what brought on that speech you gave yesterday about being thankful? And why did you all of a sudden feel the need for me to say grace over the food? Seemed kind'a out of character for you."

The trail boss looked off into the distance and shrugged. "I don't know. When I saw you helping birth them calves it reminded me of my mama. Mama raised me and my three brothers all on her lonesome. She was a strong woman who loved the Lord, but all her prayers couldn't keep my pa out of the saloon. She's gone on to her reward now." Reinhardt glanced at her and grinned. "Pirates, huh? Guess I should have brought my saber. So what kind of booty are we talking about?"

"Oh, I don't know…whiskey, rum, weapons maybe. I've heard stories that smugglers are still doing it to this day. That's why I don't want to cross over at night."

"Sounds like a good enough reason to me. All right then, let's get going." He slapped his horse's reigns and hollered, "H'ya!"

18

The rushing Gulf waters flowed through the pass into Galveston Bay.

At Sarah's urging, Pedro and Inez passed safely to the other side before the cattle.

Ginger quivered and shook her head.

Rex ran a back and forth pattern at the water's edge barking in frustration.

"Reinhardt!" Sarah held up a fist to stop the herd. She nudged Ginger's flanks and pulled her reins toward the pass. The water moved quickly, but the tide hadn't reached its full height. But if the howling wind was an indicator, high tide would be substantial.

Reinhardt shouted over the din of the rising tide and restless cattle. "What do ya say, boss lady?"

The three vaqueros draped the newborn calves across their horse's backs. The two mama cows stayed close to their bawling babies.

"All right, let's do this."

Reinhardt signaled to his flank man, Ramon, and the other two vaqueros took his lead, whooping and hollering to coax the herd into the water. The cattle moved slowly, mooing their protests to the fast-moving current. Even Rex's incessant barking couldn't get them to move quicker.

Come on go faster. You're not going to make it!

"They ain't moving fast enough. You need to do something." Reinhardt yelled.

"What do you want me to do?"

"Dang it, Sarah, use your head! Pick up that rifle and crack off a shot!"

Rex's hackles accentuated his deep throaty growl.

Reinhardt raised his fist.

Rex barked wildly at him.

Sarah pointed to the opposite shore. "Rex, go!"

The dog barked, jumped into the water, and swam across the expanse.

I don't know what's going to happen if I fire my gun, Lord. She put her hand on the rifle and froze. *Please…tell me what to do. Peace descended, despite the noise.* She fired a shot.

The cattle mooed frantically and moved faster, deeper into the pass. Panicked, some cows on the far edge cut away toward the bay instead of crossing.

"Reinhardt!" Sarah screamed at her trail boss.

"I see 'em! H'ya!" He whipped the reins. The horse galloped to the stragglers. "Ramon, Benito, aqui!"

The two men rode toward Reinhardt. The calves bawled. The vaqueros followed Reinhardt's lead, riding out past the wayward cows. With their lassos, they whipped the water and hollered.

Most of the stray cows returned to the herd.

It's working. "It's working!" Sarah cried out.

The cattle, her cattle, tromped past and into the rushing current.

Reinhardt and the two vaqueros stayed at their heels, hitting the water with their lassos to keep the cows moving.

The third vaquero made his way to the front of the herd to ride point.

Sarah rode to the far side of the pass where Rex waited.

Reinhardt and his two men were in the most danger of being sucked into the bay.

And then Benito was caught by a rogue wave. The young vaquero held onto his horse for dear life. The newborn calf slipped out of the ropes into the Bay. The mama cow's huge body acted as an anchor, saving Benito and his horse from toppling over. The new mama bit at the waves trying to rescue her calf. The water swirled, taking them both under.

Sarah opened her mouth to scream, but nothing came out.

Benito spurred his horse and followed the wet cattle out of the pass. By the time the men reached shore, the water had risen to their horses' withers. Benito pulled off his hat and shook water from it.

"Look, there's four more! Get out there and save them!" Sarah hollered and pointed.

Reinhardt rode to her and wiped his brow on his shirtsleeve.

"What are you waiting for? Go!"

"What do you want me to do, Sarah? Ride out there and drown?"

"I want you to go get my daddy's cattle, that's what!"

"It's too late. We can't save them now."

The four cows fought in water that had grown too deep for them to walk.

"If you won't get them, then I will!" She raised her hands to whip Ginger's reins.

"Oh, no, you don't." Reinhardt grabbed Ginger's halter. He held tight as the big horse shook her head and whinnied.

Sarah's chest heaved.

One by one the four cows disappeared beneath the

waters in Galveston Bay.

There was no stopping the tears falling down her cheeks. She turned to Reinhardt, "How could you?"

"I'm sorry, Sarah. I made you fire that shot. It didn't work out quite the way I thought it would, and I apologize. But we had to do something to get the cattle across the pass." His apologetic voice angered her more.

"Listen to me, old man. I'll make sure you never drive cattle again!" Her anger raged out of control at herself and at Reinhardt. She'd lost some of Daddy's cattle.

"Look at me, Sarah." Reinhardt's voice was rough. "If we hadn't got them cattle moving we could have lost half the herd. It's better to only lose a few. Now get ahold of yourself and let's get these cattle moved out of here!"

Ignoring him, Sarah pointed toward the trail and called out to the lead vaquero. "Vamos, Benito!" She spurred Ginger's flanks and took off.

"*!Arre, arre!* Whoop, whoop!"

The two other vaqueros followed his lead.

The herd began moving down the road, the pass fading behind them.

19

They stopped at Gilchrist for the rest of the day so they could make a fresh start in the morning.

This drive had been the longest, hardest and most intense three days Sarah had ever experienced.

Inez stood over a huge kettle and stirred.

Sarah didn't feel like eating, but her body needed food.

Benito had one of the men rub down all their horses. The other was feeding and watering them. It wasn't long before the crockery jug came out. They passed it around to each other and spoke loud and enthusiastically in Spanish.

Reinhardt had disappeared in the darkness.

Sarah just wanted a good night's sleep. Tomorrow afternoon they would reach High Island. She could sell off the herd, get the money, and go home. No more cattle drives. No more Reinhardt…forever. She leaned her back against a large piece of driftwood. A long groan came from deep inside. It felt good to relax, with nothing but the salty air in her lungs, and the soft sound of waves crashing on the distant shore. She closed her eyes.

A foreign noise blasted.

"What was that?" She sat straight up.

Rex barked.

It sounded sort of like a foghorn, but they were miles away from the lighthouse. *Sounds more like a goose.* An engine? But no trains were coming.

Rex's barking didn't help in the confusion.

The cows became restless, their mooing and stamping of their hooves almost drowned out the other noises.

In a cloud of sand and dust the source of the cacophony came into view. A gloved hand reached outside the rolling menace and squeezed a big black bulb. A loud honk sounded with each squeeze.

Benito and his men ran around the herd trying to calm them.

A few steers crashed their horns together and snorted, ready to fight or flee.

"Who or what in tarnation is that?" Reinhardt yelled.

"Well, I'm not expecting anyone. Are you?"

"Oh, it's one of them automobiles." He released a long low whistle. "Ain't never seen one of them before."

Pedro left Inez to finish cooking and joined them. "What's going on, Miss Sarah?"

"I don't know. It's some crazy fool, I'd say!"

Sarah and Pedro waved their arms in the air to get the driver's attention. "Stop, stop, you idiot!"

The driver finally stopped honking. He drove up close to the herd, cut off the engine and jumped out.

The herd rustled around but began to settle as Benito and the others crooned at them.

The dust and dirt settled.

Lord, I can't take much more. Has this…this person come to rob us?

The man wore a long, French riding coat, a tweed newsboy cap, goggles, and a smile the size of Texas. "Miss McKinney, I've found you." Frederick Chessher exuded pride, shucking off the leather gloves.

He pulled the goggles off, revealing those emerald-green eyes that haunted her dreams. She scowled at him. "Frederick Chessher! What were you thinking?"

"Well, I…"

"You scared the cattle out of their wits!"

"I certainly didn't…"

"Were you trying to start a stampede? Do you have any idea how bad that could have been?" Sarah stepped closer, indignation making her movements stiff.

"No!" Frederick raised his hands in defense. "I…I didn't, I don't! I mean…I'm sorry!" Every ounce of confidence seemed to melt out of the man.

He had no idea what he'd done. Sarah's anger deflated. She glanced from Frederick to his automobile, and then back at him. "Frederick, what in the world are you doing here?"

"Why, I was looking for you, of course."

"Looking for me? But why?"

"Why? Because I wanted to see you, that's why." Frederick took her hands in his. "I needed to know you were all right. I was concerned about you being out here…all alone."

"As you can see, I'm far from being alone." She swept her hand out toward the others. "I have all these people with me, not to mention all the cattle."

"I suppose you're right about that." Frederick's face became serious. "It was my hope to ride up on my steel horse and rescue you. I'd be the knight in shining armor, and you would be the damsel in distress."

Sarah could feel her eyebrows pinching together as she stared at him. "Look, I do just fine all by myself.

I don't need anyone to rescue me. Besides, you have no business being here. Don't you have a girlfriend back in Beaumont?"

"Oh, don't get me wrong, I agree with absolutely everything you're saying. But you simply must believe me when I tell you that I've tried desperately, diligently, with everything in my power, and still, I can't get you out of my mind."

The green abyss of his eyes rendered her speechless.

Frederick brushed her cheek with the back of his hand.

And every ounce of the hardcore exterior she'd built up blew away with the Gulf breeze.

20

The sunset was breathtaking. Oranges, pinks, yellows, and blues were mixed together on heaven's vast canvas.

Supper was finished, and Pedro helped Inez put things away.

The vaqueros were passing around the brown jug, their laughter growing louder as the evening went on.

Reinhardt kept his distance during supper.

Frederick was glad.

"Come sit with me." Sarah hooked arms with Frederick.

Rex followed close behind.

She led him to a big piece of driftwood, sat on the sand, and patted the ground.

Frederick waited for Rex to sit, glanced down at his trousers, and sat beside her. "Here we are then."

"Hope you don't ruin your trousers."

"Oh, no worries. I would happily pay the price for new slacks to be close to you."

She smiled and picked up a stick to draw figures in the sand. This Sarah McKinney was very different from the one he'd met in Galveston. She was in her element here. Not encumbered by layers of lace and satin and niceties. This side of her was attractive to him in a different way. She was formidable on the outside, and yet vulnerable underneath.

"I'm really sorry for the way I yelled at you earlier.

It's just that something terrible happened back at the pass."

"I'm the one who should be apologizing—flying into your camp, yelling and honking the horn."

"You didn't know any better. It's all right." She grasped his fingers.

"And for that, I'm sorry as well."

"For what?" Sarah continued to hold Frederick's hand.

"I'm sorry for being so ignorant about the ways of cattle and such. It makes me abhor being raised in the city."

"Oh, don't be silly." She lowered his hand to her lap. "You know about things I've never heard of. Besides, I'd like the chance to teach you about raising cattle."

"Well then, I might have to give you the chance." He squeezed her hand and smiled. "Tell me, how has the drive been so far?"

"It's been tough. Really tough." She retrieved the stick. "It's not easy being the lead woman on a trail drive." The sand curled with every stroke of the stick. "Especially when my trail boss initially had no respect for me and neither did his hired hands."

"I'm so sorry to hear that. What a pigheaded man. Doesn't he know it's 1900?"

"Aw, it's not a big deal. Everyone has been a big help to me, including him, and his three men. He's developed a bit more respect for me after all the things we've been through on this trip." She blew out a long breath.

"Well, I'd like to put Mr. Trail Boss in his rightful place."

She put a hand on his forearm. "Relax tiger. I can

handle Reinhardt on my own."

"You'll tell me if you need help, right?" He pumped his arm making his muscle bigger. "I was, after all, the Harvard University Boxing Club welterweight champion of 1897."

Sarah giggled, released his arm and leaned back against the log.

Frederick looked up to the heavens. The enchantment of twilight was upon them. "Oh, look, the first star." Frederick reached for her hand. "Hurry, make a wish."

Sarah closed her eyes, giving Frederick the perfect opportunity to gaze on her beauty. When she opened her eyes, she caught him looking at her. Color crept up her neck, and she released his hand.

"Sarah, I hardly even know who you are, but I must confess. Ever since your uncle introduced us, my life has been turned upside down. You are like a beautiful goddess with blonde hair and cowboy boots." Frederick took a lock of her hair in his hand. "I thought I was in love with Eliza, but if that is so, then why can't I get you off my mind?" He ran his fingers down the full length of the strands of hair.

"Please believe me when I say that if I'd known you had a lady friend I never would have come to Galveston." She sat up straight. "I'm not that kind of girl."

"Oh, heavens no. I would never think such a thing about you."

Sarah batted her eyelashes as her cheeks glowed red. "You do know I only came to Galveston to see you, don't you?"

"To be honest, I had no idea." Frederick chuckled. "Thankfully, my Harvard education kicked in, and eventually I figured it out."

They shared a hearty laugh and took turns drawing in the sand with the stick.

Frederick put his hand over hers, grasping the twig. He guided her hand and drew a heart in the sand. She looked at him. He wanted so badly to hold her body, to touch her. He took a deep breath and continued speaking. "I'm on my way to Beaumont, you know."

"Oh?" Sarah sounded out of breath.

"Yes. I have a legal matter to tend to for your uncle." Frederick continued to hold her hand and guide the stick. Her face was so close to his they almost touched.

"Important business?"

He could feel her breath on his cheek. "Yes, it is…quite important. I also have some loose ends that need to be tied up. I'm afraid that business might not have such a happy ending."

Sarah trembled. "I'm sorry to hear that. I love a good happily ever after."

"As do I, my dear." He touched her cheek to his. There was only a glow left from the sun. "Tell me, Sarah, what did you wish for?"

"I wished you would kiss me."

Not being one to disappoint, Frederick made her wish come true.

21

Sarah wiped grit from the corners of her eyes. The sun barely peeked above the briny Gulf. She stretched three nights worth of sleeping on the ground out of her stiff back. The camp was still quiet, except for the cattle grazing and waves lapping softly on the shore.

Frederick had slept in his automobile.

He looked so handsome, his spectacles pushed up to his hairline, and his arms crossed over his chest. Sarah stroked his stubbly cheek. He took her hand in his and planted wet kisses on her fingers, without opening his eyes. Sarah burned with desire to press her lips to his.

"Good thing it was me standing here and not Reinhardt." Sarah pulled her hand to her cheek.

"I'm relatively sure that Mr. Reinhardt wouldn't awaken me by caressing my cheek." He winked at her and folded his arms behind his head. "You know, you're even gorgeous first thing in the morning. I could get used to that."

A flush warmed her cheeks. "I hate to say this, but we're moving the herd out right after breakfast. I'm determined to make it to High Island today. I'm ready to have this all behind me."

Frederick sat up straight and grasped her fingers. "I understand. You've been through a lot, and I'm sure you're ready for a break."

She squeezed his hand. "And I think it would be

best if you leave before we do. I don't want that contraption of yours to cause a stampede." She bowed her head and grinned. "Freddy."

"Freddy?"

"May I call you Freddy?" A playful lilt danced in her voice.

He pulled her close. "You can call me whatever you desire, just please, don't stop calling my name." Frederick covered her lips with his in a kiss she wished would never end.

~*~

Pedro helped Inez clean up after breakfast and load up the wagon.

Benito and the other two men made preparations for the last leg of the journey. The cattle bawled and tried to scatter, anxious to get underway.

Reinhardt approached the vehicle where Frederick and Sarah were saying goodbye. "So, Frederick…" He enunciated each syllable of the young man's name. "Looks to me like you found yourself a good, strong woman."

Frederick chuckled. "Is that so, Mr. Reinhardt? I must say she's the first lady cattle baron I've had the pleasure to meet."

Reinhardt dipped his chin low. "I tell you what…you better not do anything stupid or you'll hear from me."

"Reinhardt, it's not like that!" Sarah scolded him.

The cowboy chuckled and nodded his head. "Whatever you say, ma'am." He turned and walked toward his horse.

Frederick jumped inside the automobile and

pulled on his driving gloves. "Well, I suppose I must take my leave now."

"I wish you didn't have to go."

"Oh, I do too, Sarah, but I really must take care of some nasty business in Beaumont."

"I understand." She tilted her head. "Will you be coming back through Bolivar or will you take the route back to Galveston?"

Frederick bounced his palm on the vehicle's steering wheel. "The automobile belongs to Eliza's father. It's brand new, actually. Shipment came through Galveston. I'm going to Beaumont to deliver it to him."

"Oh, I see. How will you return?"

"I will take the express train back from Beaumont. It will bring me directly to Bolivar. Quite serendipitous, wouldn't you say?"

Sarah smiled. "I would, if I knew what that meant."

"It means that I'll see you at the ranch on my way back home." He playfully put his finger on the tip of her nose. "So let's not say goodbye. Let's say, until I see you again."

"I like that idea."

"Sarah…I'm going to tell Eliza that I cannot marry her."

"Oh?"

"Yes. It wouldn't be right when I'm clearly falling in love with you." Frederick brought Sarah's fingers to his lips and kissed each one.

She had words she wanted to say, but they wouldn't come out.

"Until we meet again, Sarah McKinney."

"Yes, until we meet again." Sarah backed away

when Frederick started the engine.

He drove away at the expense of the cattle's peaceful grazing. They settled once the machine was out of sight, although dust still swirled in the air.

God, thank You for listening to me. Her heart ached for Eliza and the pain their actions would cause the other woman. *Ease her heart, God…perhaps find another person more suited to her. Because I've fallen in love with Frederick too.*

22

The cows were taken from the holding pen and lead up a ramp into long, slat-sided cattle cars.

It was over. She had done it.

A man wearing a black leather vest and a bushy mustache shook Sarah's hand. "It's a pleasure doing business with you, Miss McKinney. Your daddy, God rest his soul, had a reputation for raising some of the best Longhorn cattle in South Texas. And I'm proud to take them off your hands."

Pride welled up in Sarah at the man's compliment toward herself, and her father. "Thank you, Mr. Ainsley. I appreciate your kind words."

Mr. Ainsley pointed to a man sitting in the back of a buckboard conducting business from a small table. "Over there's my bookkeeper. He'll pay you what we agreed on."

Sarah tipped her hat and went to collect her due.

Reinhardt waited with the vaqueros and the horses. He flung a saddlebag over his shoulder and met her halfway. "You get what we came for?" Reinhardt questioned.

Sarah pulled a wad of bills from a sack and counted out the payment for him and his men.

He sucked on his teeth as he thumbed through the stack.

"Seems everything is in order. Suppose my business here is done. Unless you have more work for us, that is." He shoved the bills back into the sack and stuffed it into a saddlebag.

Sarah would miss the old coot. She smiled. "No. That's all I have." She folded the bank notes back into the sack and slid the wad into her pocket. "Say, Reinhardt, I want to thank you for all your help. I did a lot of growing up on the drive, and I have you to thank for it."

The old cowboy was clearly embarrassed by Sarah's words. He threw the saddlebag back over his shoulder and put one hand in his pocket. "Aw, well, I can't get over how much you remind me of my mama—the way you're always praying. And you're so strong, just like her. And that's a good way to be."

Heat rose in her cheeks, but she extended her hand.

Reinhardt took it. "It's been mighty nice working for ya, Miss Sarah."

"So, what's next for you, Reinhardt?"

He released her hand. "Well, me and those boys are gonna head on over to Beaumont and see what kind of trouble we can get into."

Sarah put both hands on her hips as they shared a laugh. "Now don't you get yourself into too much trouble!"

"I don't plan to." Reinhardt turned and sauntered to his stallion, giving a two finger wave. "Goodbye, Sarah!"

Rex barked incessantly at the man he never quite saw eye to eye with.

Sarah joined Pedro and Inez waiting with their donkey and cart. She mounted Ginger. "You ready?" She asked the older couple. The three of them, along with Rex, headed toward Bolivar.

~*~

The car bounced over rocks and plunged into holes the entire way. Frederick wasn't proud of his driving skills. He would have to work on them in order to keep up with the current changes in transportation. Thankfully Sarah hadn't seen him ride a horse because he was no better at that. *What was I thinking, falling in love with a girl like Sarah? I'm not the kind of man for her. She needs a cowboy, not a city lawyer who knows nothing about cattle or ranching.* Frederick shook his head and ran his fingers through his hair as it blew in the breeze. His thoughts of Sarah extinguished when the most recent problem he faced flashed across his mind. *Oh, Eliza. How will you take the news that there will be no ring, no engagement, no wedding, no…us?*

A thought more chilling than telling Eliza was how her father would react to the news. Frederick hoped he wouldn't be home and he could do the deed without the man butting in. What if he was there? What would he do to Frederick and Frederick's career?

~*~

Sarah rode Ginger ahead of Pedro and Inez's cart. They had been through much over the past few days, and there was no need to push it. She was glad for the leisurely pace. It gave her some much needed time to think. They had lost a few head of cattle, but it wasn't enough to change the amount she received. She was as tired mentally as she was physically.

The best part was Frederick showing up. His plan to rescue her was absolutely adorable. She could live with surprises such as that in her life. Every woman secretly wanted a knight in shining armor, especially one who could kiss like Frederick. She swooned at the thought of his lips on hers. *But you're not supposed to be my knight. Who am I to stand in the way of another woman's dreams of happiness? Why does it have to be this way? Why did I fall in love…with you?*

No matter what happened in Beaumont, she was determined to stick to her original plan. She would ship her father's breed stock to Uncle Jeremiah's place in Houston, and then she needed to find a ranch of her own. She was anxious to get away from the Gulf Coast and all the crazy storms her family had weathered. The blizzard that blew through in February of 1899 was completely unforeseen and out of the ordinary. It was in June of the same year that they lost cattle in a huge flood. Sarah looked out toward the waves rolling in from the Gulf of Mexico and nodded her head. *Yes. I've got to get away from here. Lord only knows what could happen next.*

23

Sarah descended the stairs and followed the smell of griddlecakes cooking in the kitchen.

Mama stood before the stove, bowl of batter in one hand and a spatula in the other. Her sisters were nowhere to be found. Since returning from the cattle drive three days ago she'd spent untold hours catching up on the chores that were left undone. She was happy to see that none of her animals had died from starvation. "Good morning, Mama."

"Morning, Sarah."

"Looks like you've been cooking a while by the size of that stack of cakes."

"Yep, takes a lot of food to feed all my kids."

"Why aren't Louise and Grace in here helping you?" Sarah took the bowl and spatula from Mama. "You go sit down. I'll finish this."

"Thank you, honey." Mama didn't sit. Instead, she went to the cabinet and proceeded to pull down dishes to set the table for breakfast. "The girls are in the living room tearing my Sears Catalogue to pieces planning for my grandbaby and for Grace's wedding." She laughed halfheartedly and shook her head. "That's the only thing on our minds here lately."

"Well, I have more important things on my mind, Mama."

"Now what could be more important than my grandbaby?" Saying the word put a smile on Mama's face.

"I'm going to Galveston right after breakfast to talk to Uncle Jeremiah about shipping the breed stock to his place in Houston."

"Oh? Will you go alone?"

"Yes, ma'am. I'll be back this evening. I've already finished the morning chores. I'll tell Melvin to check in with Pedro this afternoon. If he has the time, that is." Sarcasm coated her words, and she wasn't proud of it.

"Now, Sarah, don't be like that. And watch what you're doing. You're about to burn breakfast."

Sarah scooped up the griddlecake and flopped it onto the pile with the others. "I'm sorry, Mama, but those three act as if this is some kind of hotel, when there's plenty they could do to contribute around here."

"Oh, speaking of contributing, Melvin asked that you move the rest of your things into Grace's room. It's getting crowded in your old room with the new baby bed and all."

Sarah's blood boiled. Not only was she doing the lion's share of the chores, she had to clean out her room for Louise and Melvin. Unwilling to make the move into Grace's bedroom, she had been sleeping on the couch ever since they'd showed up. The least Melvin could do was offer to help move her things. She plopped the final cake on the pile and turned off the fire. Taking one of the griddlecakes, she rolled it up and began to eat.

"Sarah, wait until we're all seated!"

"I'm not sitting down, Mama," she mumbled. "I'm leaving. The longer I stay, the angrier I get. So I'll just go." She grabbed one of the cups of milk Mama had set out on the table and drained it.

"Oh, Sarah, please don't leave in anger." Mama pleaded.

"Mama, I love you more than you'll ever know, but this...this...*situation* ain't working out for me. I got a bad attitude, and I don't want you or anyone else to be the brunt of my anger. The sooner I get my cattle moved to a place of my own, the better off everyone will be." Sarah walked out the kitchen door letting the screen slam shut. It pained her to no end that she was the reason Mama was crying. But there was nothing she could do about that. Something had to change, and if it had to be her then so be it.

~*~

Frederick drove the automobile up to the Broussard home and set the brake. He was greeted at the door by Rachel and shown into the parlor. He sat in his usual chair—the one with the maroon and gold stripes—and waited for Eliza to grace him with her presence.

Eliza made her grand entrance and barked orders at Rachel. She waited at the door for Frederick to come to her.

He took her hand and began walking toward the seating area, only Eliza didn't move. He frowned. "What is it?"

Her bottom lip stuck out in a pout. "What, no kissy?"

Frederick begrudgingly kissed her cheek and pulled her to the chairs.

Goodhearted Rachel came to his side and poured out a glass of tea.

Frederick sipped his sweet tea and listened.

"Oh, Frederick, you're not going to believe this. Claire and Joseph are engaged! I thought I would be the next one to announce my engagement." Eliza released an audible sigh. "Oh, well. I suppose it will happen when it happens."

Eliza, I don't know how to tell you this, but I realize now that I'm not in love with you.

"I so wish you had been here over the weekend for Dorothea and Blake's wedding. She looked like a princess in her white gown." Eliza laughed wickedly. "From what I've heard she had no business wearing white. If you understand my meaning."

Frederick understood completely.

I hate to interrupt you, Eliza, but there's something I simply must tell you. Over the years I have come to know you better. And the more I do, I realize what a boorish oaf you are. I have to admit that I have no intentions of marrying you. Not now, not ever. Frederick stifled a laugh. That was rather harsh.

"So tell me, Frederick, what exactly did you say you were here for? I wasn't expecting you for another week. You do remember Sybil is getting married next weekend?"

I don't love you. Did I ever love you?

"You silly man, now you'll have to make another trip." Eliza fluffed her long skirt. "Oh, well, not to worry. Actually, I'm glad you're here. Now you can escort me to Papa's dinner party this evening."

Sarah…I'm in love with Sarah. There's nothing you can say that will ever make me love you.

"Oh, this is wonderful!" Eliza clapped her hands together.

Rachel ran through the door. "Yes, Miss Eliza?"

Eliza tightened her lips. "For heaven's sake! You

don't have to come running every time I clap my hands, Rachel!"

"Are you sure? Because the last time you clapped your hands and I didn't come a running, you was plenty mad at me."

"You're dismissed, Rachel."

Frederick covered his smile as she backed toward the door.

"Yes, ma'am, Miss Eliza."

"Servants!" Eliza shook her head. "Now where was I? Oh, yes, the dinner party. This will give you the perfect opportunity to meet with some of the town's elite. I can't wait for you to meet…"

"Stop!" Frederick held his hands up, palms toward Eliza. "Please, stop talking for one minute so that I may speak."

Eliza's mouth hung open. "Excuse me! All you had to do was say something."

Frederick sighed. "I'm sorry, Eliza, but there's something I really must tell you."

"Well, go on then. What is it?"

"This is difficult for me to say. And I'm sorry, but I must tell you." Frederick bowed his head and clasped his hands together between his knees. He raised his head and looked at her. "Eliza…it seems I've fallen in love with someone else."

She bent her head to the side, and her eyebrows came together. She sprang to her feet, not saying a word. Rage smoldered in her eyes. Her hands coiled into fists. "Who is she?"

"Well…"

"Is she someone I know?"

"No, she's…"

"When did this happen?"

"It's…"

"How long were you planning on leading me on? Have you no feelings?"

"I, I…"

"What's her name?"

Frederick stood, striking his own intimidating pose. He'd had enough. "I'd rather not say!"

Eliza's cheeks glowed a bright hue of crimson. "It's over between us, Frederick." She began to shake, her anger apparent.

Frederick closed his eyes a moment and extended his hands. "Eliza, listen to me. I'm so very sorry it happened this way, but you couldn't actually think we had a future together, did you?"

"Get out!" She pointed toward the door.

Frederick did exactly as he was told.

Rachel scurried to meet him at the door. She held his overcoat and hat, a sweet smile lit up her face. "I sho is gonna miss you, Mr. Chessher."

"Thank you, Rachel." Frederick accepted his coat and shrugged it on. "You've always shown me great kindness, and I appreciate that."

"Aw, it ain't hard being nice to someone like you." Rachel rubbed the brim of Frederick's hat. She leaned in to whisper to him. "I'm just glad you is gettin' out while the gettin' is good."

Frederick chuckled softly and leaned down, whispering back to her. "And I hope you will someday have the opportunity to get out as well." He winked at Eliza's housekeeper, and she plopped the fedora on his head.

"Maybe someday, after you marry yo sweetheart, I can come and work for you."

He tipped his hat and smiled as she shut the door

behind him.

Frederick's mind reeled. What would happen when Mr. Logan found out he'd cost him an important, wealthy client? But there were two things Frederick knew for sure. He was madly in love with Miss Sarah Jane McKinney, and he needed to purchase a train ticket back to Bolivar because he certainly wouldn't be returning in Mr. Broussard's snazzy automobile.

24

Friday, September 7, 1900

Mama's grandfather clock chimed, and Sarah sat up straight. "Three o'clock. I give up." She swept the covers away and swung her legs to the floor. She grabbed her robe off the bedstead.

It was good she'd shipped the breed stock days before. Strong winds and thunder rattled the windows all through the night.

Grace's bed was empty.

"Come on, boy."

Rex jumped up, barked, and then wagged his tail.

"Let's go see where Grace has wandered off to."

Rex ran to the bedroom door with Sarah close behind.

She walked down the dark staircase to the kitchen.

The whole family was gathered around the table. Louise sat on Melvin's lap. She didn't look comfortable with her arms draped around his neck and her big round belly lurching to one side. He gently rubbed her back. She had complained about her back pain since Sarah returned from the cattle drive.

"Hey." Sarah sat down at the table. "Is everything all right, Louise?"

"She's fine…probably tired, is all. But no one is getting back to sleep tonight." Grace yawned.

Rex sidled up to Grace and nudged her hand

trying coaxing a head scratching.

Mama fiddled with a box of matches. "Storm's coming in. Gonna be a big one. I can feel it in my bones."

"Oh, Mama, you're so full of your superstitions." Grace stretched. "What will you think of next?"

Mama's eyes narrowed. "It isn't a superstition, Grace. Wait until you get old and get the rheumatism and you'll see what I'm talking about."

"Well, that's just it, Mama. I don't plan on getting old."

"Suit yourself, but it's a might better plan than the alternative."

Everyone chuckled.

Melvin stopped rubbing Louise's back. "I don't know about everyone else, but I'm starting to get hungry. Anyone up for cooking us some breakfast?"

Sarah, Grace, and Mama turned to look at Melvin as if they'd rehearsed it. The only thing that saved him was the flash of lightning that lit up the entire house for a brief moment.

Rex barked from his hiding place at their feet.

Louise tightly grasped Melvin around his neck.

Grace put her hands on the table and sat up straight. "All right y'all, brace yourself for it."

A low rumble rolled in, increasing in intensity as it drew near. The windows rattled so hard it seemed they would fall out of their frames.

When the thunder ceased, so did Rex's barking.

Sarah put her hand on his head for comfort…his *and* hers.

Mama pushed away from the table with a sigh. "Might as well cook some breakfast." She turned to the one man in the room. "Name your poison, Melvin."

He smiled at his mother-in-law. "Griddlecakes please. And…hold the poison."

After breakfast, dark gray skies loomed overhead. Rain began to come down.

Sarah fed the animals by lamplight before pulling boards, nails, and a hammer from inside the barn. She knew right where everything was, having helped Daddy secure the house from storms many times in the past. The wind blew out the lamp. She pulled down her cowboy hat as she walked to the house. The rain and wind had picked up, and it stung when it hit her face. Inside the kitchen, Mama scrubbed the breakfast dishes while Grace dried and put them away. The other two adults weren't around.

Sarah put the lamp on the sideboard. "So where's Princess Louise and Prince Melvin?"

Grace giggled, but Mama whipped her head around and snapped at Sarah in a loud whisper. "Now don't you talk like that. Those back pains Louise is having means that baby is gonna come soon. And it ain't time for it to come yet. I don't want you doing or saying anything to upset her!"

"Yes, ma'am." Sarah's sassiness took over again. "It's just that they hardly ever do anything to help around here, Mama."

Mama pointed a finger at Sarah. "I'm sure you'll tell me if I'm wrong, Sarah Jane McKinney, but if memory serves, this is still my house. And as long as I live here, I'll be the one in charge. Do you understand me?"

"Yes, ma'am."

"Now until that baby is born, you, and me, and Grace can do the lion's share of the work. Melvin is a grown man, and I ain't his mama. He can see what needs to be done all by himself." Mama went to wipe off the table.

"I'm not so sure about that," Sarah mumbled under her breath.

"Excuse me?"

"Nothing, Mama."

Sarah was thankful when Grace drew their mother's attention away from her. "Mama…" She waited until a loud thunderclap passed before continuing. "If you don't mind, can I go over to the lighthouse and check on how they're doing over there?"

"Are you finished putting away the dishes?"

"Yes, ma'am."

"All right then, go on ahead. But be careful out there. It looks nasty."

"I will. Thanks, Mama."

Sarah twisted her lips to the side as her sister walked out the door.

There goes another pair of helping hands.

"Mama, we need to get the windows boarded up before the storm gets here."

"All right, go on and do it. You know what needs to be done."

"I need help. Can I have your permission to ask Melvin to help me?"

Mama abruptly stopped wiping. "Don't get all surly with me, Sarah. Go tell Melvin you need his help. And hurry up about it."

"Yes, ma'am."

Louise and Melvin sat reading books.

Sarah took a deep breath to quell her anger. She put her hand on Melvin's shoulder.

"Yes?" He said, looking up at her.

"Melvin, there's a big, bad storm brewing outside."

"Why, yes, I have noticed."

"Oh, good. Well, here at the ranch we board up the windows when a big storm is coming."

Melvin returned her cynical smile. "Is that so."

"Yes, yes, it is. That's why I've come to ask for your help."

"And what is it that you want from me?"

"Actually, I thought you would have taken the hint by now. But since you haven't…would you please get off your lazy rump and come help me board up the windows before we all get blown to kingdom come?"

Melvin jumped to his feet.

Louise gasped and dropped her book. She put one hand over her mouth and one on her tummy.

Sarah headed out the door.

The only thing Melvin understood was a good, swift kick in the rear end or his wife's baby sister telling him what to do.

"Sarah Jane McKinney! Get in here right this instant!" Mama's voice was shrill.

Her shoulders slumped. *When am I ever going to learn?*

25

Frederick hadn't slept so well in a very long time. He got out of bed and threw back the draperies allowing the bright light to come inside. "What a beautiful day!" He opened the window of the second-floor hotel room. The wind sent dirt flying into his eyes. He slammed the window shut and went into the bathroom to splash water on his face. Everything he did was from a fresh point of view. He even shaved his beard with renewed energy.

He was free from Eliza Broussard. Free from the controlling grip she kept on him that was tighter than the knot in his tie. He was free to make his own decisions. He planned to use his newfound freedom to finish his business in town and get away from Beaumont, Texas as fast as he could.

His heart was in another place, Bolivar Peninsula, where the most beautiful girl in the whole State of Texas was hopefully waiting for his return. Straightening his jacket, he considered his image in the mirror. "You're looking rather dapper this morning, Frederick." With a chuckle, he grabbed his fedora from the hook by the door and left his hotel room a new man.

The stiff blowing winds kept shop owners from leaving their doors open.

Frederick held onto his hat as he looked for somewhere to get a bite to eat.

The Jefferson Diner, perfect. Eliza loathed diners. Frederick pushed open the door. A quaint bell jingled overhead. "Ah, lovely. Eliza would have hated that."

Inside the diner, he took a seat at the counter and turned over the coffee cup. A woman with a pencil stuck through a knot in her hair came and filled the cup. She took an order pad from her apron pocket and removed the pencil. "What can I get ya, hon?"

She called me hon, how quaint. Eliza would have called for the manager by now. "Yes, ma'am. May I have the two egg special, please?"

"You sure can, hon." She scratched his order on the pad. "What kind of meat you gonna have?"

"Fried ham, please."

"Uh huh." She made another scribble. "And how do you like your eggs?"

"Over easy." Frederick put his thumb and index finger together. "Very easy."

"No problem. Toast or biscuits?"

"Hm…" Frederick tapped his chin. "I believe I'll have toast."

"Sounds good. Anything else I can get ya? Juice? Milk?"

"No, thank you." He smiled.

"All right, then."

"Oh, wait, one more thing," Frederick called out. "Will you also bring some strawberry jam, please?"

"You got it, hon!"

Frederick picked up the morning paper someone left behind. *Look at me now, Eliza. I'm reading a used newspaper. What would you think of me now?*

News of the upcoming election was splattered across the front page. The war in the Philippines took up a good amount of space. One story near the bottom of the page caught his eye. *West Indian Hurricane Skirts Western Florida.*

Frederick shifted his gaze to the diner's window. It wasn't even raining, but a strong northeastern wind continued to build. Trees waved back and forth.

The Weather Bureau office in New Orleans, Louisiana has reported heavy damage along the coastline. The National Weather Bureau in Washington, DC has ordered storm warnings from Pensacola, Florida to Galveston, Texas. No evacuations are called for at this time.

The waitress served Frederick his breakfast with a smile on her face. "I haven't seen you around before. Are you new in these parts?"

"Oh, no, ma'am, I'm in town on business." Frederick surveyed his food. "Thank you."

"I see. You in town for long?"

"Uh, no, actually. I'm traveling back to Bolivar on the G&I tomorrow morning."

"Be careful out there with that storm coming in. They don't know where it's going, but I have a feeling it's gonna be close to us."

"If the storm does come to Beaumont will it harm the rest of the coast, say Galveston or Bolivar?"

"That depends on how big a storm it is. That's what's so bad about living near the coast. You never know what's gonna hit you. It could be just a little rain and wind, but it might be like the one down in Indianola back in eighty-six. It destroyed the whole town and killed more than seventy-five people."

"Oh, my."

"Yeah, the people there gave up trying to rebuild. It's deserted now."

"That sounds absolutely horrific."

"Um-hm. It was. All right, you enjoy your

breakfast."

Looking out at the storm, Frederick was anxious to get on with his business and get out of town. He was taken aback by an overwhelming desire to be with Sarah, to hold her in his arms, to protect her, no matter the cost. A life without Sarah would be no life at all.

26

Sarah pulled her hat down tight. She tied a rag over her face, covering her mouth and nose to keep sand and dirt out.

Melvin did the same.

They all chuckled at Louise's comment on how they looked like a pair of wimpy bandits, but when she grasped her round belly and winced in pain it was no longer a laughing matter. The house had to be protected for the baby's sake.

Pellets of rain peppering Sarah's skin felt like buckshot. "Pick up one of these veneer boards and follow me!" Sarah shouted over the howling wind.

Melvin lifted one end and helped drag it to the front of the house.

They covered the window.

"You go ahead!" Melvin said, struggling to keep the board in place. "I'll hold it while you nail it to the wall!"

Sarah hammered a nail into one side and then did the other side so Melvin could let go.

"Come on, Sarah. Let's get the next one."

The wind was stronger than Sarah ever remembered in the past. The downward gusts were unrelenting. "I'll get this one," she hollered.

Melvin took the hammer and nails.

She lifted the veneer and held it between her outstretched arms. A fast-moving gust caught the board like a sail. The wind carried her a good five yards before the board flew out of her hands leaving shards of wood embedded in her palms. She fell into a puddle of mud. The board kept going—straight toward Melvin. "Get down!" She screamed.

Melvin dove just in time. The veneer passed over his head before it crashed into the house, leaving a gaping hole.

Sarah jumped to her feet and ran to her brother-in-law. "Melvin! Melvin!" She pulled the rag down from her face and knelt beside him. "Are you all right?"

"Yes, I'm all right. Just a bit shaken up."

Tears streamed down her raw cheeks. They were both soaking wet and covered in mud. Her breath came in short gasps. "You could have been killed!"

"But I wasn't. I'm fine." He took a deep breath. "What about you, are you hurt?" Melvin removed the rag tied around his face and wiped mud from his eye.

"No. I don't think so. My backside will be sore tomorrow though."

Melvin pointed to her hands, dripping with blood where the veneer had slashed her skin. He wrapped his bandana around her hand, then used hers around her other hand.

Her lips began to tremble.

Melvin patted her arm. "It'll be all right. Let's get this over with."

Sarah grabbed his hand. "I'm really scared, Melvin."

He shook his head. "I know. I am too."

A thousand pounds of guilt perched on Sarah's head for the rotten way she had treated her brother-in-law and everyone else. No one worked hard enough to please her, and nobody was as good as her daddy. She had grieved her father's death by making everyone around her miserable. God had to use a storm, a flying board, and mud puddle to get her attention, and He'd done a fine job of it. Sarah wept and shook with fear. She looked into her brother-in-law's eyes. "I'm so sorry for the way I've treated you, Melvin. I expect every man to be my hero like my daddy was, and that's not fair to you or anyone else. Daddy said these boards would protect us." She gasped for a breath. "But he was wrong. You were nearly killed, and we can't even get them hung!"

Melvin squeezed her shoulder. "Calm down, Sarah. It's all right to idolize your father. He was a great man. But he was just a man. The only one who can help us now is God!"

Sarah pressed her face into Melvin's chest, trying to be heard through her sobs. "Will you please come help me with the animals?"

"Of course."

Together they fought the violent wind.

"Then we'll figure out a way to protect ourselves inside the house."

"Thank you, Melvin!"

"You're welcome. And by the way...I accept your apology!"

27

Saturday, September 8, 1900

Frederick awakened early following a restless night. Worry concerning Sarah and the coming storm filled his mind. He rushed through his morning routine and packed his suitcase. After checking out, he headed for the train station.

An older man with thick white hair, mustache, and sideburns stood behind the barred window with the words *Ticket Office* embellished above it. "Next!" The man called out.

"Yes, one ticket for seven o'clock on the G&I to Port Bolivar." Frederick handed the man the required fee. "Thank you, sir."

"It's gonna be a bumpy ride to Port Bolivar. What with that storm coming in."

"Is it projected to be a big one?"

"Yep."

Frederick got on the train, worry about Sarah consuming his thoughts

"All aboard!" The conductor gave the final call for passengers.

The whistle blew as the engineer released the brake. The engine lurched forward. The billowing clouds of steam and smoke were whisked away by the blustery winds. Trails of raindrops slid across the windows. The engine built up a head of steam and chugged out of town.

Goodbye, Beaumont. I hope I shouldn't have to return anytime soon.

A man in front of him was talking about the storm to his companion. Frederick tapped him on the shoulder. "Have you heard anything about the storm coming in? Have there been any reports as to where they think it might hit?"

"I don't know, young man. But if you listen to what the animals are saying, it'll be a big one. I've lived on a farm and raised animals all my life. If you know animals like I do, you'd know how they can predict the weather. Take cattle for instance. If you see cows laying down in the field, and then you can bet your bottom dollar that rain's coming. And watch the birds. If they're flying low to the ground…"

Frederick nodded politely and tuned out, his worry for Sarah increasing by the minute.

28

"Careful, Melvin! You're gonna break that lamp."

Mama was in a tizzy. She hollered at poor Melvin and Sarah nonstop as they moved things to the second floor.

A neighbor stopped by earlier, on their way to the ferry to warn them of the fast-rising tide from the storm surge.

Sarah recognized Mama's actions. She'd seen it before when Daddy was gored by Brutus. "Mama, leave him alone. We're doing the best we can." Sarah spoke softly to distract her mother. "Why don't you go to the kitchen and gather some canned goods into a box. And anything else you think we might need. We may be up there a while."

A clap of thunder rattled the windows and lightning flashed in every corner of the room.

Rex ran down the stairs nearly knocking Melvin off his feet.

Mama nodded at Sarah before walking away.

Sarah couldn't stop worrying about Frederick. It seemed like eons since she'd seen his face or touched his hand…or kissed him. He said he would come back to Bolivar. Maybe he couldn't get back. Or perhaps he'd changed his mind. *Was that Your plan all along, Father?* A grain of hopelessness settled in her heart, took root, and started to grow. *It doesn't matter, Lord. He wasn't mine to begin with.*

She pulled back the sash from one of the windows they hadn't been able to board up and looked outside. It was difficult to see past the property line with the rain coming down in sheets. The wind blew as though it had a purpose.

Something hurtled toward the window, and Sarah stepped back as a seagull crashed into the glass with a sickening thud. Rex barked wildly. The bird slid down the cracked glass before a gust of wind picked it up and whisked it away.

Sarah dropped the curtain and clutched her blouse, gasping. *Oh, Father, God. I don't know my future with Frederick. I don't know if I even have a future with him at all, but please, Lord, please…keep him safe.* She pulled back the shade again.

Two figures fought their way through the wind and rain. Sarah ran to the door and opened it. Once the couple was inside the door, Sarah shoved her weight against it until it latched.

Grace and Grace's fiancé, Guy were soaked through. Water formed a puddle on the floor. Grace wept and shook, Guy's arm tightly draped around her shoulder.

Sarah pulled a throw off the back of the couch and drew it over Grace's back.

"Sarah, Uncle Harry received a telegraph, and this storm…" Guy used his hands in an emotional plea. "It, it's bad, really bad. We could barely get here from the lighthouse. The water is coming up fast. He said he's never seen it like this before."

"What's going on, Sarah? Is someone here?" Mama came in from the kitchen, holding a box. She put the crate on the floor and rushed to Grace's side.

"Mama!" Grace bawled, falling into her mother's

arms.

Melvin ran halfway down the stairs. "Who was at the door? Is everything all right?"

"Listen to me, Mrs. June, Uncle Harry said to get y'all over to the lighthouse right away. Now we've got to hurry before the tide rises any higher." Guy shook his head, his hands extended before him. "It's now or never!"

"I don't know what to do. We've got to get our things upstairs."

"It's no use, Sarah!" Guy hollered. "We've got to get to the lighthouse now. It's our only hope."

Louise…the baby. They had to get out fast. The baby's life depended on it. "What do you need me to do?" Sarah asked, determined to get her family to safety.

"You help your mama gather up food. Oh, and candles if you have them." A low rumble of thunder rattled the window frames. Guy gathered Grace to his side and looked at Melvin. "Get your wife down here now. We've got to get everyone to the lighthouse."

Melvin scrambled up the stairs.

"Come on, Mama."

"Stop!" Mama put her hands out and planted her feet. "I'm not leaving this house. We've been through many a storm before, and this ranch has survived 'em all. There's no point in running off when everything we need is right here."

Sarah froze.

Melvin whirled around.

Guy extended his hand to Mama. "Mrs. June, please!"

"No! We're not leaving!"

Sarah took Mama by the arm and led her to the

picture display on the sideboard. She picked up the small gold frame and handed it to Mama.

Even in her state of panic and shock, Mama managed a small smile. She rubbed her thumb on the photograph next to the baby's cheek.

"Who is that, Mama?"

"Well, it's Louise, of course. Don't you think I know my own baby when I see her?"

"I'll bet you Louise and Melvin's baby will look just like her…you think?"

"I sure hope not. Louise had a head shaped like an oil funnel. I wouldn't wish that on my precious grandbaby!"

"Mama…we've got to get Louise and the baby out. It's too dangerous for them to stay here. Now you don't want anything bad to happen, do you?"

One by one, Mama grabbed the photographs of Grace and Sarah off the sideboard and added them to the one already in her hand. She rushed over to the crate of food she'd gathered and placed them inside. Putting her fists on her hips, she turned toward the stairs. "Melvin, go get Louise! I've got to get my grandbaby out of this house!"

Melvin ran up the stairs.

Mama picked up the box, trotting back to the kitchen. "Sarah, Grace, get ready to go."

"Yes, ma'am," Grace replied.

Guy gave Sarah an amazed look. "Good job."

"Don't thank me yet. We still have to get her out of here without taking the whole house."

"Sarah, I need you in the kitchen!"

Thinking of things to save, Sarah rubbed her hand against the bulge in the pocket sewn into her skirt. It was still there. "Coming, Mama!"

29

The rain was making visibility through the train's windows impossible. Frederick had no way of knowing how bad things actually were. The train was rattling more than usual as gusts of wind slammed against it.

"Whoa!" A little girl screamed when the train lurched yet again. "Mommy, I'm scared!"

People were talking loud, trying to drown out the noise.

"I'm not quite sure, but I think we passed right by the High Island terminal without stopping," A young Negro man seated in front of him said.

"What? Why wouldn't they stop the train? Surely there were more people needing to board." Frederick asked. A knot gripped Frederick's stomach as he stood up. He got no more than six steps away when the train shot forward. The impact sent Frederick down to his hands and knees. The other passengers were tossed about, and varying groans and startled screams filled the air.

Frederick rushed to the window to look outside. Water lapped against the side of the train. Rainwater or seawater? Probably both. Apprehension rose in his chest.

The forward door opened from the outside. The conductor climbed inside the car and snapped the door shut. He swiped his cap off and wiped rain from his eyes.

For a brief moment, the passengers silently stared at the man.

"What's going on? Why did we stop?" A portly man's words were tinged with anger.

The conductor held up his hands. "All right, now, quiet down and listen. We have a situation here we have to deal with."

"What kind of situation?"

"All right, here's how it is. We're not far from Port Bolivar. That's the good news. The bad news is that the train stalled out, and the water is continuing to rise. I figure we're about eleven miles from the ferry."

Comments rumbled through the crowd of passengers.

"What does that mean to us? How do you propose we get to the ferry landing to get back to Galveston?" The portly man spoke again.

A troubled look came over the railroad worker's face. He gripped the seatback in front of him. "That's another problem. If the waves are this bad inland, I can only imagine how bad they must be at the ferry. In the past they've stopped running the ferry when the weather is bad like this. I don't know. If it were me, I wouldn't want to risk it."

"So what do you propose we do?" someone demanded.

"Well, the engineer suggested we all hunker down and wait it out."

Frederick could stay onboard the train and wait out the storm, but staying meant he had no way of knowing the fate of Sarah and her family. "Excuse me, sir, but do we have the choice of leaving the train…to seek shelter elsewhere?"

"Sure, I suppose you could leave, but why risk your life out in this storm when you're safe and sound right here in this sturdy train?"

Murmurs came from all around the train car.

"All right, now listen to me. The engineer is doing everything he can to get the train back up and running. Then we can back the engine toward Beaumont and out of this mess." He removed his cap and wiped his forehead with the back of his sleeve. "All right, those are your choices. You can wait it out here, or you can leave and face who knows what." He flipped his hands up and walked toward the door.

Frederick gripped the seat. Should he take his chances in the storm? What if Sarah needed him? Sure, she lived in a sturdy ranch house, but was anything strong enough to withstand a storm of this magnitude?

A palm frond glanced off the side of the train and slid down the rain-soaked window.

He had to get to Sarah.

30

The storm was like nothing Sarah had ever experienced. Greenish-black clouds boiled in the sky overhead. The rain came down in sheets that drenched her to the skin. She had to stay strong for Mama and her sisters, especially Louise. It was too soon for the baby to come into the world.

Guy helped Melvin lift Louise into the back of the cart.

Sarah hitched Ginger to the front.

Louise screamed again that the baby was coming, then the pain would pass, and she would quiet down for a moment.

Mama climbed up in the wagon and sat behind Louise, supporting her back.

The closer they got to the lighthouse the less jarring the ride became. The storm surge rose to the point where the wagon was floating. Rex tired from swimming and jumped up into the wagon. He lay down beside Louise and whimpered.

Sarah held Ginger's reigns as they waded through the deep water.

How on earth would they get Louise all the way to the top of the one hundred twenty-foot tower?

The lighthouse door opened and Guy's uncle appeared holding a lantern. He rushed to the wagon. "Let's get her upstairs."

Somehow the three men managed to get Louise up

the stairs.

Grace grabbed the box of supplies and followed Mama up the stairs.

Sarah unhitched Ginger from the wagon. She was glad for the rain to hide her tears as she removed Ginger's bridle and halter. Ginger nickered and nuzzled Sarah's face. Sarah kissed her horse's muzzle and rubbed her neck. "Goodbye, beautiful." Sarah shut the lighthouse door.

~*~

Frederick pleaded with the elderly man in front of him. "Sir, I implore you to come with us. The water is rising fast. I…I don't feel it's safe to stay here."

The old man patted his wife's knee and smiled. "Thank you, but there's no way we could make it out in this storm. Lana and I will stay right here until it passes."

"But, we can help you." Frederick gestured to the young woman standing beside him, who'd opted to leave with Frederick. "Please, it's no trouble."

The man offered his hand to Frederick. "No, no, we'll stay. Besides, I've always liked sitting back and watching a good storm. Look here…we have front row seats."

Frederick stood and motioned to the people who stood with him, the woman, her daughter, and the young Negro man. "Listen up, everyone. We've all been given a choice to either stay on the train or leave and seek shelter elsewhere. These people have all made the decision to leave with me. I know of a place near here where we can wait out the storm. Does anyone else want to go with us?"

A man called out. "You're crazy if you go out in this storm! You'll never make it to wherever you're going!"

"I'm sorry you feel that way, but I don't think it's safe here for any of us. I'm getting this young woman and her child out of here. You're free to come with us if you'd like."

"Lady, I think you're making a big mistake going with this man." He held his arms out to the little girl. "Come on now little lady. Stay here with me."

The child frowned and pressed her face into her mother's skirt.

"Fine, then. You go on with that crazy man."

Frederick took hold of the woman's arm and led her and the child to the train's door. Another man who'd decided to go moved in front of them to open the door.

"Hold up!" A man bellowed.

Another man jumped from his seat and pulled his son up by the arm. "We're going with you!"

~*~

The room beneath the lighthouse's lantern was called the gallery. It was a completely round compartment with one door that led outside to the catwalk. It was large enough, but with Mr. and Mrs. Claiborne included, there were a total of eight people gathered inside…and one tail-wagging dog.

Sarah thought some of them would clear out since her sister seemed on the verge of having the baby. But no one seemed anxious to leave.

"Over here we have about a month's supply of food." Mr. Claiborne pulled Sarah, Grace, and Guy aside. "Now come over here." He indicated for them to look out a small window overlooking the catwalk. He pointed out to a bucket hanging from a hook. "That bucket is for collecting rainwater, but the wind is blowing too hard to catch any."

Mrs. Claiborne prepared a comfortable pallet for Louise. "Now let's have her lie down here."

Mama and Melvin helped Louise down onto the pallet. Melvin sat down and held his wife's head in his lap. Mama knelt beside Louise.

Mr. Claiborne spoke to his wife. "I saw people wading through the tidewater coming this way."

Mrs. Claiborne nodded. "Guy, Grace, let's go downstairs and see what we can do to help."

"Sarah, I need you to stay here with me," Mama said.

"Yes, ma'am."

Rex followed the others down the stairs.

Louise screamed.

Mama leaned in to assess the situation.

Sarah rushed to her sister's side and held her hand. "Mama, I know you know what you're doing, but I can help when it's time for the baby to come. I've helped cows give birth. I even helped a newborn calf take its first breath when I was on the cattle drive."

Mama chuckled. "Oh, well, if you've helped birth a calf then your little niece or nephew should be a piece of cake for you."

Louise looked at Mama and Sarah with fire in her eyes.

Melvin panicked. "Louise, honey, now you need to sit back and relax, darling."

Louise's head snapped toward her husband. "Shut up, Melvin!"

"Mama, Sarah…you better listen close because I'm only gonna say this one time! I am not a heifer, and my baby is not a calf!" The poor girl grabbed her belly and cried out in pain. Liquid dampened the pallet beneath Louise.

"I need you to find something sharp I can cut with." Mama directed Sarah. "And get those swaddling blankets out of Louise's bag."

"Yes, ma'am." Sarah squeezed Louise's hand before collecting the things Mama needed. Despite her experience with cows, it was difficult not to be afraid for her sister and the baby.

31

"There it is!" Frederick shouted to the small band of people walking behind him. The McKinney ranch house came into view. He'd carried little Alyssa all the way from the train. The water was too deep for her to walk.

Theodore, the young Negro man, helped Emily, the girl's mother, wade through the thigh deep water. John and his son, Nelson, followed behind them.

Frederick trudged on toward the front porch. There was at least a foot of water covering the wooden veranda. The wind cruelly picked up anything and everything in its path to hurl their way. The rain blew sideways and stung when it hit.

Emily screamed, and Theodore gasped.

Frederick turned around. Emily was nowhere to be seen. Alyssa screamed for her mother. Frederick held her tight.

"Now look what you did, you idiot!"

Theodore's eyes were wild with panic. He slashed at the water with both hands—searching and pulled the young woman up by her arm.

She held on tight while she coughed and spat seawater from her mouth. "Please, don't let go! I've hurt my leg!"

Theodore scooped her up, cradling her in his arms. She put her arms around his neck and laid her head on his shoulder.

The men waded through the water. The screen door hung from one hinge.

Frederick banged on the door with his fist, but no one came. "Sarah! Sarah! It's Frederick! Open up!"

There was no answer.

He tried the door. The wind grabbed it and pushed it open, sending a wave of water into the living room. Frederick looked around and moved inside when Theodore came up behind him, holding Emily. The floor was covered with seawater.

"Sarah! Are you in here?" He turned to Theodore. "Bring her into the kitchen. We'll lay her out on the table, and I'll take a look at her leg." Frederick sat Alyssa on the counter. He leaned down and spoke softly to her. "I need you to stay right here while I look at your mother's leg."

"All right." She nodded, on the verge of tears.

Frederick grabbed a lamp and rummaged through drawers until he found matches to light it.

"Oh, there you are." John entered the kitchen with Nelson, his son, following.

"Set her down here," Frederick said to Theodore.

Theodore gently set Emily down on the table.

She winced.

"Mommy, I'm scared." Alyssa held her hands out toward her mother.

"Stay right there, Alyssa. We'll take care of your mommy." Frederick's heart raced. He wished Sarah was home. She was raised on a ranch and knew so much more about…everything.

John Hobbs leaned against the counter. Nelson boosted himself up onto the counter.

Frederick worried they might have come along for the sole purpose of mischief towards the others. He had to stay on guard for all of their safety.

"Ma'am, what happened?"

"I don't really know. My foot went down into some kind of hole. The water pulled me under, and I twisted my ankle." Tears flowed down her face, and she shook with cold, and probably, a touch of fear.

Theodore stepped forward. "May I take a look?"

"Um, do you mind, ma'am?" Frederick asked.

"Just please, one of you do something," she pleaded. "My leg hurts so much."

Theodore gently pulled Emily's skirt up to her knee. She wore high-heeled boots, laced up to her calves. "I mean you no harm. I'm a doctor."

Frederick was caught completely off guard. "You're a doctor?"

"Yes, sir," Theodore answered.

The kitchen wall shook when something big crashed against the house. The wind played havoc with the equipment left outside.

"Mommy!" Alyssa cried.

"It's all right, baby! I'm right here."

"Ma'am, I have to remove your boot." Theodore spoke to his patient. "I apologize, but this might hurt."

"I'm ready, go on."

The doctor unlaced the boot, and the young woman winced in pain.

Frederick cringed at the contorted angle of her foot.

Theodore pulled Frederick aside. "She has a serious ankle fracture. I'll need your help to set the bone."

Enormous drops of rain splatted against the kitchen windows.

Frederick spoke in a low tone. "Since we arrived

the water has risen several inches in this kitchen."

"Do you suggest we move upstairs?"

"My friend who lives here grew up on the peninsula. She and her family know this area better than anyone. And that they're not here tells me they didn't feel safe here. I have a good feeling they've gone to seek shelter in the lighthouse. They know the light keeper. It's tall and strong. They would be safe there."

"I don't think we should move Miss Emily. That ankle is badly broken."

"I understand, but I'm afraid if we stay all of us might die."

A window shattered somewhere in the house.

"We won't be safe here for very long."

"All right. Give me a hand, and we'll see how she's doing after I set the bone." Theodore turned. "Miss Emily, I have to move that broken bone back into place. Now, Frederick, I need you to stand over here and hold Ms. Emily's leg firmly while I do this."

Theodore began to adjust the bones.

Emily moaned, and tears ran down her cheeks.

"All right now, Miss Emily, I'm just about done. Take a deep breath."

Theodore quickly snapped the bone back into its proper position.

Emily screamed in pain.

"There we are. All done."

"Mommy!"

"Bring her to me," Emily gasped through her tears.

"Go ahead, but don't you move that leg," Theodore instructed. "I've got to find something to wrap it with."

Frederick picked up the little girl and placed her

on the table with her mother.

Theodore rummaged through the kitchen.

"Listen up now." Frederick addressed the others. "Theodore and I have decided to take Emily and Alyssa to the lighthouse. You can stay, or you can go with us. It's your decision."

The older man pulled back his coat. He removed a small handgun and pointed it at Frederick. "You see that's where you're wrong. None of you are going anywhere until I get what I want."

32

Frederick raised his hands and moved away from the others. "All right, now, put down the gun and tell us what you want."

Emily squeezed Alyssa tight and whispered into her ear.

Theodore continued to wrap Emily's leg and secured the rags he'd found in a drawer with twine that had been in the same place.

"You listen good. This is the MK Ranch. I saw the brand on the gate we came through. I'm familiar with the cattle these people produce, and I know how much the MK beef stock goes for on the market. These people are rich, and I plan on taking some of that money off their hands. Now tell me where the safe is!"

"I don't know what you're talking about. I know the people who live here, and they are by no means rich!"

"Look here, anyone who is friends with an uppity lawyer would have to be well to do. So tell me where they keep their money."

"First of all, the man who owned this ranch is dead. The only people left are his wife and daughters. If they have any money, I certainly don't know about it." Frederick's eyes narrowed to slits. A man who took advantage of good people in their most desperate moment was deplorable. "If you think there's a treasure to be had then why don't you go on and search for it?"

"That's not a bad idea." He turned to his son. "Come on, Nelson. Let's go take a look around. Grab that lamp."

The younger Hobbs jumped down. Water splashed around him. He took the lamp and waded behind his father out of the kitchen.

Something crashed into the house overhead.

Alyssa screamed.

Frederick lit another lamp.

The sound of water streamed through the house. Their fortress had been breached. Staying was a sure death sentence. They had to leave…it was now or never.

"Theodore, Emily, we've got to get to higher ground. I don't think this house can withstand the storm."

The doctor gestured to Emily. "How can we possibly move this woman with her leg fractured and only strips of cloth for protection?"

"Not to worry. I have an idea."

Emily pulled her daughter to her chest. Sweat formed on her forehead, and her arms were shaking. "What about those horrible men? What if they see us trying to leave and shoot us?"

"Please, you must calm down and listen to my plan."

Theodore pulled Frederick aside. "What's your plan? We need to get her to safety. I fear she's going into shock."

"Theodore…" Frederick shook his head. "How rude of me. I apologize…Dr. Freeman…can you lift Miss Emily onto the counter while I remove the legs from this table? We can move it outside and put the ladies on it." Frederick raised his hands, palms up. "You know, like a boat of sorts."

Theodore turned to his patient. "I need to lift you onto the counter for a moment while our friend here prepares for our departure."

Emily stared at the doctor, her coloring fading. She handed Alyssa over with trembling hands.

Theodore moved them both before turning to Frederic.

Fredrick flipped the table upside down. "Give me a hand will you, doctor?" He used brute force to knock off three of the legs. The last leg proved to be a problem, and he decided to leave it be. "Stay here with the ladies until I get this table out the front door. I'll call for you directly."

"Wait! We need to gather a few things."

Frederick wrangled the table, floating on top of the water collecting in the kitchen. "What do we need?"

"Blankets. We need to keep Emily warm. And we need bindings as well."

Frederick pushed the table toward the doctor and left the kitchen. A loud thump against the side of the house awakened Frederick to the need for the bindings. It was the best way to keep Emily and Alyssa from being blown off the makeshift boat. He strode through the deepening waters trying to find something that could be used for a strap. Where had he seen a rope?

Mr. McKinney's lariat rope and hat were on display in his honor near the row of coat hooks by the front door.

Frederick grabbed the rope and took the hat as well. He wedged the Boss of the Plains Stetson hat on his head. The pride the family took in the items lent to his renewed vigor to place the hat in the hands of the ones it rightly belonged to.

Frederick and the doctor pushed the tabletop through the waters out onto the front porch. They placed Emily and her daughter on the raft, bundled in blankets and tied against the remaining stubborn table leg.

"All right, ready to go."

A large hand clamped down on Frederick's shoulder and swung him around. "Wait right there. You're not going anywhere!"

Frederick didn't release his hand from the table. "What do you want, Hobbs?"

"I want to know where the McKinneys keep their money. That's what I want!"

"I told you, they don't have any money!"

"Don't give me that! I don't believe you!"

The gun came closer to Frederick's face. He reached deep into his trouser pocket. His hand emerged holding a wad of bank notes and silver coins. "If it's money you want then here, take it!" Frederick threw the money. The bills unfolded as they flew over the two men's heads.

The elder Hobbs was caught off guard.

"I'll get it, Daddy!" Nelson dropped the lamp and dove after the coins and notes.

The room was plunged into darkness.

"No, you idiot, you'll drown!" Mr. Hobbs hollered. He thrashed around searching in the dark water. "Nelson, Nelson! Where are you?"

"Go now!" Frederick and the doctor pushed the table. It floated off the porch. The water was up to Frederick's chest. He looked back, but couldn't see anything in the darkness. They guided the makeshift raft away from the ranch.

In the distance, Mr. Hobbs mournfully cried out for his son.

The wind blew so hard it was nearly impossible to keep the raft on course. They bounced up and down on the waves. The land had become sea. Frederick swam to keep his chin above water. Dr. Freeman was doing the same, when Frederick glanced his way as lightning flashed. Miss Emily and Alyssa were huddled in the blankets, but occasionally he could hear the little girl's cries over the roar of the water. He was thankful for the darkness because of the death and destruction floating around them.

Sarah had to be inside the lighthouse. Its tall beacon guided him onward through the briny depths. Frederick shuddered when a bolt of lightning struck the roof of a small farmhouse. The entire sky illuminated. A quick glance revealed a body draped across the house's front porch stairs. A smaller figure floated nearby. Frederick turned his head in anguish. He spat saltwater from his mouth and refused to pray for help.

Why would God allow this to happen?

33

A white bolt of lightning slashed the sky like a fiery sword. Sarah cringed, waiting for the thunder. In an instant its fury was unleashed in a loud, explosive blast. A low rolling rumble followed, rattling the huge tower windows above the gallery. Over one hundred feet in the air was a terribly frightening place of refuge during the massive storm.

"Mama! Mama! Another one's coming!" Louise screamed and leaned forward. Sweat slid down her crimson cheeks.

Grace's arms were wrapped tightly around knees pulled up to her chest.

Sarah hugged Rex.

The lighthouse stairs began filling with weary storm survivors.

Mama placed her hand on Louise's round belly. "All right, honey. You just squeeze Melvin's hands as hard as you can. It's almost time to push. Just hang in there a little bit longer, sweetheart."

"You're doing a great job, Louise." Melvin squeaked the words out.

Sarah moved from Rex's side and knelt by Mama at the business end of the birth. She handed Mama whatever she asked for, vowing never to get pregnant as long as she lived. She'd heard how beautiful and natural the birth process was supposed to be, but after this day she would question that notion. It was one thing to watch a cow give birth. Seeing it happen to one's flesh and blood sister was another thing all together.

"Oh! Oh! Oh! Oh! Oh!" Louise hollered with each panting breath.

"That's right, honey, blow it out. That pain means the baby's almost here. Don't push yet, all right?" Mama's voice cracked and a tear rolled down her cheek.

Wind hit the lighthouse with unrelenting gusts. Sarah was knocked over from her kneeling position.

Louise released a bloodcurdling scream followed by heart wrenching sobs.

Rex whimpered from where he sat across the room with Grace.

"Shh, shh, everything'll be all right." Melvin stroked his wife's hair away from her face.

"Mama?" Sarah whispered, half panicked. "Is she going to be all right?"

"She's ready. Tear a strip of cloth from that rag. Make sure the knife is close where I can find it, and put those baby blankets right here." She patted the floor beside her.

"I've got to push!"

Mama put her hands on Louise's knees. "Don't push yet, honey, just one more minute. Sarah, get over there with Melvin. I want one of you on each side of Louise. Get your shoulder in behind her so she can push against you."

For the first time since Daddy died, the strong, brave woman her mama used to be returned. God was there with them.

Mama rubbed Louise's knee. "Well, Melvin, are you ready to be a daddy?"

"Ready as I'll ever be."

"All right now, honey, whenever you're ready you can start pushing."

Louise didn't waste any time. She planted her feet and pushed. Her body went limp. She panted; exhaustion was setting in.

"Come on, honey! Push! I can see the head!" Mama spoke firmly to her daughter. "I need you to give me one more big push so we can get this baby's head out."

"I don't want to do this anymore," Louise cried in anguish, shaking her head. "I can't!"

"Well, you don't have any choice." Mama looked at Sarah and Melvin. "When the next pain comes, I'll count to three, and you two help her push. Ya hear me?"

"Yes, ma'am," Sarah answered.

Melvin nodded and sniffed; his eyes brimmed with tears.

"It's coming!" Louise yelled.

"One, two…three, push!"

"Good, good! Keep going a little more!" Mama called to Louise. "The head is out."

Sarah craned her neck for a glimpse of the baby's head. A reddish orb covered with dark wet wisps of hair came into view. Perhaps the baby looked like his side of the family.

"You're doing a wonderful job, my love. I'm so very proud of you," Melvin said.

Lightning filled the room with white light. The clap of thunder followed. It no longer drew their attention as it had before. There was a more important matter at hand.

"All right, now, honey, it's time to get this baby

out. Give me one more big push!" Mama instructed.

Louise released a deep, throaty holler, her face scrunching up.

"Good girl, Louise…push!" Mama yelled.

And seconds later, the baby was born.

Louise collapsed against Sarah and Melvin.

"Is everything all right?" Melvin's voice was anxious.

The baby's cry was a soft little noise that was barely heard above the raging storm.

Mama looked up with tears streaming down her face. "It's a boy."

"Give him to me." Louise held up weak, shaky arms.

Mama quickly put him on the blankets. She used the topmost blanket to wipe him off. His cries grew louder as she rubbed his tiny body.

Gazing at his face brought tears to Sarah's eyes. She was an aunt.

Swaddled tightly in the remaining blankets, Mama picked him up, kissed his forehead and handed him to Louise.

Louise lay back against Melvin, and they examined every facet of their baby's little red face.

Grace looked at her new nephew. "Oh, Louise, he's so beautiful!"

Melvin gently kissed Louise's red cheeks. She reached her hand up and put her palm on the side of his face.

Sarah was moved by the love that flowed between them.

Someone knocked on the floor hatch on the floor and raised it slightly. Rex barked at the intruder. Grace motioned for Guy to come in.

Sarah went to one of the porthole-shaped windows to look out. Lightning lit up the sky, allowing a glimpse of the surroundings below. Nothing but rushing water covered the entire peninsula. Her heart grieved. She brushed tears off her cheeks and looked at her family. Louise had Melvin. Grace had Guy. Even Mama had her new grandson. Sarah was alone. *Father, please protect Frederick.* Thunder rolled, rattling the glass. She put her hand on the cold surface. *It's hopeless. No one could survive out in this storm.* Sarah bowed her head against her arm. *Oh, Lord, if it be Your will, please light the way that I might see him one more time.*

34

"There, up ahead! I see the light!" Frederick yelled to Dr. Freeman over the roaring din of the storm. He quickened his pace. It seemed to have the same effect on the doctor. Both men pushed the table raft holding the mother and child as if they were on the last leg of a most peculiar relay race.

Darkness surrounded them on every side. Objects floating in the water bumped into Frederick, unnerving him. His leg muscles burned with every swimming step. The wind pushed against the raft. Frederick had to get them to a safe place before it was too late.

And, at last, they reached the lighthouse.

Frederick stood at the door of the great tower and pounded against it, his hand burned with each blow. He tried opening it, but it wouldn't budge. Once again, he beat on the door.

Someone was opening the latch. They were saved.

A male figure stood inside the door as water poured in around his knees.

Frederick leaned in close, keeping his grip on the table. He pushed Mr. McKinney's hat up on his head so the man could see his eyes. "Sir, we are two men with a severely injured woman and her child. I beseech you to give us shelter."

The man held a lantern, illuminating his weathered, kind face. He immediately opened the door as best he could in the deep waters. "We don't have much room left, but come on in."

He helped hold the table steady while the two men untied Miss Emily and Alyssa.

Frederick held his arms out to the little girl, and she leapt into them.

The doctor lifted the young woman off the raft and carried her inside the structure.

Frederick followed with Alyssa, set her down on the stairs, and then turned to help the lighthouse keeper close the door against the flood. Other hands reached to push the door closed.

Frederick glanced out the crack in the door in time to see their raft whisked away by the rushing Gulf water.

Dr. Freeman placed Miss Emily on the stairs and sat down beside her.

She slumped against the doctor's shoulder like a ragdoll.

The man lifted his lantern and looked closely at the young woman. "Is she all right?"

Dr. Freeman nodded. "Yes, I believe she will be all right now that we're out of the storm. She's suffered a severe ankle fracture. The elements haven't been kind to us. She needs to rest."

"I can understand that. By the way, I'm Harry Claiborne, the lightkeeper."

"Frederick Chessher and this is Dr. Theodore Freeman." Frederick waved at Theodore. "Thank you so much for allowing us in." Frederick shook the man's hand while standing in the waist high water as though it were normal.

The lantern light cast eerie shadows against the brick tower wall. Every step going up the enormous tower was filled with survivors, two and three abreast.

Women and children wailed in terror as the lighthouse swayed against the relentless wind. Seawater dripped down on the newcomers from the soaking wet clothes of those sitting above them.

"Good lord, how many have you taken in?"

Mr. Claiborne stared up at the crowd above him. "More than a hundred."

A sliver of hope entered Frederick's heart. "Tell me, have you seen a young woman with long, golden hair? She would have been with her mother…and sisters."

"Mister, I have no idea who all's on these stairs. Anyone who came to us we let them in." He wiped water from his face. "I've got to get back up topside. Can't let the light go dark. It's my duty."

"Yes, of course." Frederick grasped Claiborne's arm. "Again, I thank you for allowing us shelter."

Mr. Claiborne dipped his chin. He put his foot on the step beside Alyssa and carefully made his way over, around, and through the horde of people taking refuge on the stairs.

Frederick sat down beside Alyssa. She snuggled close to him, and he pulled the child into his lap. Large round eyes stared up at him.

"Are we safe now, Mr. Fred?" Raindrops mixed with tears sparkled on her lashes in the slowly fading lantern light.

Water lapped at the soles of his shoes. He squeezed the little girl tight. "I certainly hope so, my dear."

The lamplight evaporated, plunging them into total darkness. Alyssa laid her head against his chest. "I'm scared," she whined.

"Don't be afraid, darling. I'm right here, and I

won't let go."

"You promise?"

"Yes, I promise."

"Mr. Fred, Mommy says that when I'm afraid I should ask God to protect me. Will you say a prayer for me?"

Frederick refused to acknowledge God, Who brought such hellish destruction down on His people. No, he wouldn't do it.

"Why don't you say your own prayer, Alyssa? How does that sound?"

The child huffed out a stream of sobs. "But, but, I don't know how!"

Dr. Freeman reached down and rested his hand on Alyssa's head. "I'll pray for you, child. Now bow your head."

Frederick was happy for the darkness surrounding them. It hid his quivering lips. He didn't have to conceal the burning teardrops brimming over his eyelids. No one could see his heartache. *Oh, Sarah, please be safe, wherever you are.* He couldn't quell the sobbing that shook his body. *If I die this night, my love…I, I hope you will find my lifeless body and know that I came back for you as I said I would. I love you, my darling. Please know that I love you.*

35

Sarah rubbed the chill bumps forming on her damp arms. The cyclone forced rainwater through even the tiniest crevices in the gallery walls and windows. The door to the catwalk rattled furiously. She prayed the hinges would stay in place. Should they give way, she and her family would be sucked out into the raging tempest. The skies had been dark as nightfall most of the day. If Frederick were here he could look at the shiny gold watch he kept in his vest pocket and tell her the time. Sarah closed her eyes against such thoughts. It only made the pain in her heart sting all the more. She leaned over and put her arms around Rex's neck, thankful to have him by her side.

The storm came ashore with a fury never seen before. Surges of wind pressed against the lighthouse. The enormous tower swayed like a palm tree in the unrelenting wind.

Most of those in attendance had their heads bowed. They all prayed, many out loud, that God would spare their lives.

Mr. Claiborne worked to make sure the beacon never went dark.

Sarah's heart went out to the people lining the spiral stairs. The rungs were so narrow. The desperate cries from the children expressed how terribly afraid they were in the cramped, dark confines of the tower.

They hadn't had anything to eat or drink for hours. There must be something she could do to help. *Mr. Claiborne's water pail!*

He'd drawn in the bucket of rainwater and emptied it into another container several times already. Sarah rose from the floor, careful not to lose her balance and headed for the water receptacle. Picking up the two tin cans Mr. Claiborne had previously used, she scooped water into them and went to the hatch in the floor. She opened the doorway.

A woman with wild, windblown hair squinted up at her.

"I have water, two cans full. Tell everyone to take a sip and pass it down. And send them back up so I can refill them."

The woman accepted the first can and gave a sip to the old, white-haired woman next to her. "Bless you, child." She then took a small drink herself before passing the cans and the instructions on to the persons sitting below her. "The water is salty."

"Yes, I know."

"How can there be seawater in the rain?"

"I don't know." She closed the door. Sarah crawled to Mama. "I'm so scared, Mama. I don't think we're gonna make it."

Mama patted Sarah's arm. "You've got to have faith, baby girl. God didn't bring us this far to abandon us when we need Him the most. He's gonna see us through."

Sarah closed her eyes, desperately trying not to panic. She wanted nothing more than to share her mother's blind faith, but how could she when every one of them was doomed? The inevitable was coming as fast as the impending cyclone. "But there's never been a storm this bad, Mama! And, and, what about Frederick? He said he was coming back to me, Mama! He's not gonna make it!"

Mama squeezed her tight and shushed her. "Calm down, Sarah. Everything is gonna…"

Screech!

Mr. Claiborne pulled his head out of the small closet he rustled through and turned his ear to listen.

Screech!

Rex barked wildly at the strange sound.

"What is that?" Grace hollered.

The lightkeeper turned toward her voice, but looked at his nephew. They exchanged a knowing look before he turned his gaze to the closest circular window. "That sounded like the clockworks!" He dashed to the door and peered out the circular window. "It's the clockworks all right. I don't see any rotation of the light." Claiborne put his hands on his hips and stared at the storage closet he'd previously been rummaging through. He turned to Guy. "I'm going up."

Guy released Grace and jumped to his feet. "Not without a safety rope you're not." He went to the closet and pulled out a length of rope and began tying it around his uncle's waist. He took the other end and tied it to an iron eyebolt.

Mrs. Claiborne hugged him. "Please be careful, dear."

Mr. Claiborne kissed the top of her head and scrambled from her embrace. He grabbed a couple of tools out of storage and made his way up the ladder built into the gallery wall.

Guy climbed halfway up the ladder and kept watch over him.

"Be careful, Guy!" Grace yelled to her fiancé.

"Come here, Grace!" Mama motioned her over.

Grace scooted across the floor next to Mama.

"Look!" Grace pointed to the window. Once again, the lighthouse beacon was turning round.

"He's rotating the fixture by hand," Guy said.

"How long can he keep that up? What if he can't, and a ship runs ashore? Or even worse, it crashes into the lighthouse!" Grace was terrified.

Mama began softly singing. "My hope is built on nothing less than Jesus's blood and righteousness. I dare not trust the sweetest frame, but wholly lean on Jesus's name."

Sarah and Mrs. Claiborne joined her.

"On Christ the solid rock I stand, all other ground is sinking sand; all other ground is sinking sand."

Mrs. Claiborne sang the next verse. "When darkness veils His lovely face, I rest on his unchanging grace. In every high and stormy gale, my anchor holds within the veil!"

Mama raised her hand in praise. "Amen!"

God's presence shined bright inside the lighthouse.

An unexplainable peace shown on Grace's face when His Spirit came upon her.

They kept singing.

"On Christ the solid rock I stand, all other ground is sinking sand; all other ground is sinking sand."

~*~

Water covered Frederick's legs to his knees. He held Alyssa tight. He feared she might fall into the swirling waters and drown. In the time since they had arrived, the water's depth had risen by at least three inches. He concentrated on taking deep breaths and releasing them. It was his only defense against the chilling fingers of claustrophobia closing like a vise around his neck. He had nowhere to go, neither up nor down. A hundred or more souls hung on iron rungs above him, and a dark watery grave pooled at his feet.

A deafening boom of thunder was only one of numerous noises triggered by the roaring cyclone. His eyes remained wide open even though he was enveloped by total darkness. Objects hit the tower walls. A loud thud…perhaps it was a cow or maybe even someone's bed. *Ping, ping, ping.* Had it begun to hail? Or had some poor child lost his marbles? He feared he was losing his.

The next sound made him pull Alyssa's head into his chest, covering her ears. The deep guttural sound of a man screaming seemed to go on forever. In a final, swelling crescendo, the body hit the outer wall with a sickening thump. The screams fell silent. Contempt boiled inside Frederick. "Where are You, God?"

A small hand curled around his thumb, and Alyssa pulled his hand to her chest. "Don't worry, Mr. Fred. God is right here in my heart, and He's going to protect us."

Frederick leaned his head into Alyssa's matted hair and kissed her. She reminded him so much of his two little sisters back home. Would they have been so strong faced with the same situation? Would he ever see them again? *God, if You really are here, please spare all of these gathered in this strong tower. And God…save my Sarah.*

36

Sunday, September 9, 1900

Sarah awakened to the sound of a baby crying. The lighthouse was no longer swaying. Brilliant sunbeams dotted the gallery floor streaming through the small round windows. She wiped sleep from her eyes and looked from one person to the next. They had survived the storm.

Louise remained on the pallet where she'd given birth the night before. Had it only been one night?

Grace helped Mrs. Claiborne organize their supply of food.

If the sounds coming from the lighthouse stairs were any indication, the throng of hungry storm survivors needed to be tended to.

Guy and Mr. Claiborne fiddled with the light's clockwork mechanism. Poor Mr. Claiborne laboriously turned the device by hand most of the night. His arm muscles bulged from overuse, but he had seen to it that his post wasn't vacated.

"Harry," Mrs. Claiborne called out, attaining her husband's attention. "How does it look outside?"

He went to the gallery door, unlatching it he swung it wide open. The small room flooded with light. They all shielded their eyes against the brilliance. Claiborne went out onto the catwalk surrounding the gallery and surveyed the land.

Sarah walked to the doorway.

Rex jumped up.

The lightkeeper held his hand up. "Stay back. There may be damage to the railing."

"I just want to look out." She clung to the doorframe with one hand and held Rex's collar with her other hand. The sheer destruction wrought by the storm took her breath away. A vast wasteland replaced the peninsula she knew and loved. Sand covered everything. The dunes were laid flat. The surf came farther inland than she remembered. Where was the ranch? She ran to the opposite side of the gallery and looked out a window. She turned away and slid down the wall to the floor. Where was Galveston?

Mr. Claiborne came back inside and shut the door. Mouth gaping open, he shook his head and stared at his wife.

"What does it look like out there, uncle?" Guy asked.

It was as though he couldn't collect the words to describe what he'd seen. "The water has mostly receded." He moved to the floor hatch and got down on one knee. He pulled the door open revealing the two women Sarah had passed water down to the night before. "Mind your ears, ladies." Once they'd covered their ears, Mr. Claiborne shouted down into the tower. "The tide has gone out! Open up the door!"

A smell wafted up through the hatch that rivaled the McKinney barn before the stalls were mucked. Celebratory noises rose from the stairs, but there was also wailing and crying.

No one could leave the gallery until all the people below moved down the steep spiral stairs and outside the lighthouse.

Sarah slid across the floor to join her family.

Melvin held his baby boy like an old pro.

"He's beautiful, Melvin."

A mixture of love and pride showed in the man's eyes. "Thank you, Sarah, but I think the word you're looking for is handsome." They exchanged a soft chuckle. "Would you like to hold him?"

Sarah held her hands out. The baby turned his head to her chest and made sucking motions with his tiny lips. "Hey, I'm not your mama!" Everyone laughed at Sarah's outburst.

"You must smell like his mama." Mrs. Claiborne interjected from the other side of the gallery.

Sarah gazed into her nephew's eyes. "You should give him a name like Stormy or…or Gale. You know, because he was born in a storm."

"Sarah, no, that's just silly." Mama wasn't thrilled.

"His name is Melvin. But I do like the name Gale." Louise looked up at her husband. "Don't you, Melvin?"

"He certainly deserves a commemorative name after all he's been through." Melvin hit his knee with his fist. "It's settled then. His name shall be Melvin Gale Culp."

Sarah handed him over to Louise. Rex sat down beside her.

Golden sunlight continued pouring in through the small round windows. It was a miracle that none of them had broken during the storm. Several of the large glass panes surrounding the lantern room above them had shattered in the night.

What would Mama do when she found out the ranch was completely gone? Mama had already given up on cattle ranching anyway. But where would they all go?

Mr. Claiborne returned to the floor hatch and lifted it open.

Guy walked over beside his uncle and looked down the shaft. He turned to Grace. "It's almost cleared out below. You ready to go take a look outside, honey?"

Grace wasted no time rising and dusting her hands on her skirt. "You better believe I'm ready."

"Anyone else going down with us?"

Mr. Claiborne scratched his whiskery chin. "I need to see how bad we fared through the storm. And I have to get more fuel for the light. You going down, Mama?"

Mrs. Claiborne placed one final item into the box she'd been gathering together. She patted the container. "Yes, I'm coming. Guy, can you carry this box down for me? We have a lot of hungry people to feed."

"Yes, ma'am."

"Mama, I'm going down. Are you coming?" Sarah asked.

"I suppose so. I hate to see the mess left by this storm." She rose from the floor and looked down at mother, father, and baby. "Y'all gonna be all right without me for a while?"

Louise nodded.

The trek down the iron stairs seemed to take forever. Her heart beat faster the closer they came to the door. How much worse would it be up close?

Rex quickly trotted off, having important business to tend to.

Sarah put her hand up to shield her eyes from the brilliant sunlight. God made amends for the horror of the previous night with the most beautiful sunrise Sarah could ever remember seeing.

Mama grasped the bodice of her dress and clamped her hand onto Sarah's arm as she sank to the ground. Sarah grabbed her before she went all the way down.

"Grace, help me!" Sarah hollered.

Grace and Guy rushed over and helped Sarah get Mama back on her feet.

"Are you all right, Mrs. McKinney?" Guy asked.

Mama's face was white as a clean linen sheet. "I, I'll be fine. I just need to sit down."

Guy and Sarah helped her over to a tremendous tree trunk that had washed in with the storm. The downed tree was so enormous that Guy had to put his hands around Mama's tiny waist and lift her up onto it.

They were surrounded by death and destruction on every side.

Piteous tears burned her cheeks as Sarah stared at the senseless violence. *Dear God, what must it have been like for them?*

The lighthouse inhabitants milled about the grounds. Some turned over bodies checking for loved ones.

Sarah couldn't look at them. Why had God spared her life and her family and not these people? And if she looked, she might see his face…no. She shook her head and looked instead at all the dead animals, hoping she didn't see her loyal companion, Ginger.

A big steer lay lifeless on the ground. Several more just like it were scattered about. Moving closer, she examined the animal's hindquarter. The brand on the beast's haunch was a large T8. Sarah's eyes half closed in a squint. "Tate…"

Mr. Tate refused her any help selling off the herd after Daddy passed. He didn't get his cattle to market before the storm hit. And now they were all dead. It didn't bring her any joy.

Grace appeared by her side, tears ran down her porcelain cheeks. "Oh, Sarah, there's nothing left!"

"I know, sister. But we still have our lives, and that's more than can be said for these poor folks."

Mama rested a can of water on her crossed legs. Guy offered her a soda cracker from a box, but she waved him off.

The crackers looked as delicious as roast beef to Sarah, who hadn't eaten for hours.

Rex sat at Guy's feet whimpering for a morsel of food.

"Sarah, look at that beautiful rainbow!" Grace exclaimed.

The glorious symbol of God's everlasting promise stretched across the sky. One end reached all the way passed Bolivar, the other covered the entirety of what was Galveston Island.

"It's so beautiful, Grace. Thank You, God, for keeping Your promise not to destroy the entire earth by flood."

A large hand gently grasped Sarah's shoulder. Startled, she turned around and looked up into familiar green eyes. Her bottom lip trembled, and tears gushed. She tried to speak, but the words wouldn't come. Frederick leaned down, covering her lips with his. Sarah put her arms around his neck as they shared warm, passionate kisses. She never wanted to let go and risk losing him again.

Mama didn't share in her concern. "Sarah Jane

McKinney, let go of that boy!"

"Yes, ma'am!" Sarah giggled.

"Oh, I'm so thankful you're alive." Frederick released her and held her at arm's length.

He looked as though he'd been through so much, which reminded her of what a terrible mess she must look like. She had been so shocked by his appearance she didn't realize what he was wearing. Her hand rose to her cheek. "You're wearing Daddy's Stetson. How on earth did you come by that?"

Frederick grinned and removed the big cowboy hat. "I knew it was important to you, so I made a special trip to pick it up. And now I'm returning it to its rightful owner." He set the Stetson on Sarah's head.

The big hat slid down to her nose. She laughed and took it off. Reaching up, she set it down on Frederick's head. "It looks much better on you."

Frederick made a stern face and wiggled his eyebrows. "Why, thank ya, ma'am."

"I love you, Frederick Chessher."

"And I love you, Miss Sarah Jane McKinney." Frederick leaned in for another kiss, but was stopped abruptly.

"Hey, you two! Stop all that kissing and get over here right now!" Mama hollered.

Sarah seized the opportunity and pecked him on the tip of his nose.

He threw his head back and erupted in laughter.

Hand in hand they walked toward Mama.

Mama would scold her for their outlandish public display of affection.

But with her head floating amongst the clouds Sarah couldn't muster enough energy to care. She was in love…and her Frederick was too.

37

Frederick held Sarah's small hand as they walked toward the McKinney ranch. His life had changed in the course of one night. He had learned so much in the short time he'd spent in the lighthouse. He wanted, no needed, to think further on the things God showed him, but the utter horror of the destruction that lay before them demanded his attention. "Are you sure you want to go all the way to the ranch? It might not be safe."

"Yes. Mama wants to know how bad it is." Sarah pointed to an empty space where a house had once been. "I think that's where the Bradleys lived. I hope they made it out."

"I do too, my love." Frederick felt sick to his stomach remembering the scene he'd passed the night before. Some of them hadn't made it.

The peninsula didn't have much of a road to begin with, but now there was none at all. Still, they walked where the road had once been. Things that had once been someone's earthly belongings surrounded them, books, clothes, washbasins, dishes, a stuffed bear. Did their owners make it?

"I still can't believe you were safe inside the lighthouse the whole time."

"Well, not exactly. My friends and I were the last four people to be admitted before the lighthouse keeper shut the door."

"You brought friends with you?"

"Not friends really. They were people on the train with me. A doctor, a young woman and her little girl."

"You were on the train? Oh my, that must have been frightening."

"Yes, but not nearly as frightening as helping the doctor set a badly broken bone, or wading through waist deep water and guiding a makeshift raft to the lighthouse with a mother and child balanced on top of it."

"Frederick, that's awful. However did you manage?"

"Oh, it wasn't a big deal, I suppose. God was with us. And it was nothing like having a gun pulled on me. Do you suppose I qualify as a true Texan now?"

"What on earth happened?"

"I'll tell you all about it later. Let's go see what's left of the ranch."

The metal tracks of the Galveston and Interstate Railroad were pulled from the ground by the sheer force of the wind. Wooden crossties weighing two hundred pounds or more were tossed about like dead maple leaves in the fall.

"Oh, Frederick, thank goodness you got off the train when you did."

He nodded in disbelief, but didn't utter a word, thinking of those who'd stayed with the train.

The ranch wasn't far ahead of them. Frederick held tight to Sarah's hand. There was nothing left, not even the huge barn. No ranch house meant they wouldn't encounter the dead bodies of Mr. Hobbs and his son, Nelson, he hoped. Frederick stopped walking and turned to Sarah. "There's something I've been pondering I would like to ask you about."

"Oh, what is it?"

"Before I found you at the lighthouse I heard you talking to Grace about the rainbow. You seemed almost thankful. It...it's hard for me to fathom you feeling that way after all you've been through."

Sarah's soft smile filled his heart with joy.

"I am thankful. Didn't God keep His promise not to destroy the earth with flood? And He spared my life and my family too. I think I have much to be thankful for."

Frederick pushed the cowboy hat up and rubbed his forehead. "I'm trying to understand. Truly I am." Despite his assurance before that God was with them, he struggled with his newfound feelings, seeing the destruction around them.

She squeezed his hand. "That's all I can ask for."

~*~

Sarah ran to where the gate bearing the MK brand once stood. One lone wooden post remained. Sarah collapsed against the pole, grabbing hold of it with both arms. It was all gone, the ranch house, the barn, the animals—her home. She let go of the post. Her boots sank into the waterlogged sod with every step. A small section of the house's floorboards, the part attached to the fireplace was still there. Huge stones had dislodged from the chimney. Sarah hopped up on the elevated floor.

"Sarah, be careful!" Frederick yelled.

One of the boards twisted beneath her feet. She grabbed hold of the mantel that was still attached to the fireplace remains. The center stone was still there. "Will you hand me one of those small rocks, please?"

"You need to come down from there. It's not safe."

"I will, after you give me a rock."

"Your mother will have my hide if you hurt yourself."

"I won't get hurt. Now hand me that dark brown rock."

Frederick gave her the stone.

She pounded against the fireplace with the rock. Grunting with each glancing blow, she wiggled what she was hitting up and down, back and forth, until it came off and slipped into her palm. "There, I have it!" With a satisfied smile, she held up the wrought iron MK brand that had embellished their fireplace her whole life.

"Are you quite happy now?" Frederick put his hands around her petite waist and lifted her onto the ground.

"Yes. It's all I have left."

Frederick swallowed her in an embrace. "I'm so sorry, my love."

"It's all right. Now I have something to remember this place by."

"But it's not all right. You've lost everything. Why aren't you furious with God? I haven't lost nearly as much as you, and I am angry."

Sarah clutched the wrought iron emblem to her chest and gazed up into Frederick's gorgeous green eyes. "Everything I've lost are just things, and things can be replaced. I have my life and my family, and that's all that really matters. When I was at the top of the lighthouse during the storm, I didn't think we would make it. I prayed God would save us." She looked back at him. "I also asked God to spare your life, and look, here you are."

Frederick plopped down on the edge of the remaining floorboards. After what seemed like a long time he finally looked up at her. "Your words reminded me of something that happened while we were in the lighthouse. I heard a man screaming, but the water was already too deep. There was no way I could open the door. I didn't know where you were. I feared you dead. In my desperation, I called out to God. I asked Him to spare the lives of the people in the lighthouse." He raised his head and looked at her with watery, red eyes. "But I begged Him to save you, Sarah. I realize now…He answered my prayer."

Sarah fell to her knees. Her skirt squished into the soft earth. She held her hands out, and Frederick took hold of them. "You prayed for me?" Her eyes could no longer hold onto the tears. "Both our prayers were answered."

Frederick released Sarah's hands and wrapped his arms around her. "Oh, my darling, Sarah, I love you so."

"And I love you, Fre…"

Frederick pressed his lips to hers and stirred something deep within her. His lips slid from her mouth and caressed the length of her neck. She sucked in a deep breath as heat rose up her chest. Bells rang. Were they wedding bells? The more Frederick kissed her, the louder the bells sounded.

"Missy Sarah, Missy Sarah!"

She would know that accent anywhere.

Pedro and Inez drove their mule cart up the washed-out drive. The mule's fancy harness jingled with each step.

Sarah quickly turned to Frederick. "Is my face red? It feels very hot. Just look at me. You've made a complete mess of me."

Frederick chuckled and pulled his handkerchief out. "You're absolutely beautiful. Just as you always are." He offered her the cloth.

She rubbed her neck and face.

"Pedro! Inez! Praise God you made it through the storm!" Reaching the cart, Sarah threw her arms around Inez's neck and hugged her tight. "Pedro, Inez, this is Frederick Chessher." Saying his name ushered the heat back up her neck. She couldn't stop smiling.

"*Que paso?*" Pedro held the reins in both hands.

"*Hola,*" Inez said, a big grin on her face.

"Um, uh, hola." Frederick shoved his hands in his pockets.

Pedro rested his arm on his knee. "*Donde es su Mama, y hermanas*…uh, uh, sisters?"

Inez's eyes grew wide, and she grabbed Pedro's arm. "*El bebé!*"

"Everyone is fine. We stayed in the top of the lighthouse. Louise had the baby, a little boy!"

Inez put her palms on her cheeks and rattled something in Spanish.

Pedro looked confused and glanced from Inez to Sarah and back to Inez. "Que?"

"What is it, Pedro?" Sarah asked.

Pedro laughed, a hand resting on his round belly. "She, she say she want to know why you cheeks color so *rojo!*"

Sarah's hand flew to her cheek. She opened her mouth to speak. "I…I…" She turned to Frederick who covered his mouth with his hand. "Uh! Not you too!"

"I'm sorry, Sarah, but you are quite red."

In the past, Sarah would have stomped off, mad at all of them, but not anymore. Her life had been spared, along with her family and the love of her life. She wouldn't waste another day worrying or feeling sorry or getting even. She would live every day to the fullest, just as God had planned. She put both her palms on her burning cheeks. "Oh, my goodness! They are hot!" A wide smile spread across her face, and she began to chuckle, which then turned into a deep, body-shaking, contagious laugh.

The others joined in.

38

"How much farther do you think it is?" Sarah swatted at a large biting fly. "Oh, these infernal bugs won't stay off me!"

Frederick's smile turned into a cringing grimace when one of the bloodsuckers bit the back of his neck. "Ouch!" He slapped at the creature but missed.

They continued following the train track.

Suitcases were scattered about on the sand.

"Look over there."

"Where? What is it?"

He pointed out across the salt marsh.

"I can't make it out."

"It's the baggage car. That looks close to five hundred feet away."

"How do you know?"

"I've noticed a lot of baggage. I knew we must be getting near the train." He took her by the elbow and guided her on.

An enormous pile of sand covered the railroad track. There was something buried inside the dune.

"Do you see that?" Confusion washed over Sarah's face.

"Yes." Frederick continued walking. "This is where the train stopped."

Sarah stopped and looked at him. "Do you mean? Is that…?"

"Yes. I'm afraid it's the train's passenger cars."

Frederick took Sarah by the hand when she caught up with him. "This won't be pleasant, my dear."

A dozen or more bodies were strewn across the sand.

Sarah grasped Frederick's arm as they drew near.

They passed a woman dressed in fine traveling clothes. Her death face told of the great terror she'd witnessed. A young girl was facedown, a small suitcase clutched tightly in her hand.

Frederick heard Sarah sniff. He put his hand against her face, drawing her near. She didn't need to see any of this.

They reached the train. The cars that remained were buried in sand. The cyclone took water from the Gulf and used it to push tons of sand against the stalled train. Only the very topmost section was sticking out of the enormous mound.

Frederick grieved for the sweet old couple he'd met on the train. He struggled to remember their names…Billy and Lana Putnam. They had loved each other for sixty years, in sickness and in health. And now they were gone, entombed inside a passenger car on the Galveston and Interstate Railroad. Why did they have to die in such a horrible manner? "A lot of people died on that train…good people."

Sarah looked up into his eyes. "One didn't. I still have you." She walked ahead, and then gave a sudden gasp.

"What is it?"

She pointed to a body. He squeezed her hand.

No more arrogance, no more chauvinism, no more Laird Crosby.

"I met him on the train. He didn't know who I was, but I knew him," Frederick said.

Sarah's bottom lip quivered. "Horrible man." She sniffed and began to sob.

Frederick lifted her chin. "He won't hurt you ever again."

Tears ran down both sides of her face. "It's not that."

"What is it then?"

"I can't believe how close I came to losing you. I prayed for your safety, and God heard me. If you had stayed here, you would be dead…and I don't know what I'd do without you."

Frederick pulled her into his embrace and held her tight. "Oh, Sarah, Sarah, I'm right here." He spoke into her long, blonde hair. "I'll never leave you, my dear."

"Tell me you love me."

"I'll love you for the rest of my days on earth, and I'll love you in heaven for all eternity."

Sarah stopped crying.

He covered the top of her head with sweet kisses.

"I'll love you forever, Frederick Chessher."

"I know you do." He placed one more kiss on her. "Come on, let's get back to your family."

~*~

Monday morning, the tenth of September dawned as another gorgeous day. Those who survived the storm in the lighthouse were exhausted, Sarah included. A gloomy cloud of despair floated around the temporary camp. Many had lost their homes, but some had lost family as well. The weary troop had spent an entire night sleeping on the cold, sandy ground.

The people worked with a singular purpose, help

one another, bury the dead, and keep the fire burning. It offered them a shred of normalcy after all that had happened.

Mama had only momentarily covered her mouth with her hand and closed her eyes when Sarah told her about the fate of the MK Ranch.

Mrs. Claiborne, Mama, and a couple of the other women worked as a team preparing food from the lighthouse rations the Claibornes so generously provided.

Rex tried his best to help the women, but they would have none of it. Dejected, he joined Sarah and Frederick who kept the little girl, Alyssa, occupied so her mother could get some much-needed rest.

Sarah used a stick she'd picked up to show Alyssa how to draw in the sand. "Look what I made, Alyssa. It's the lighthouse. It's your turn now. What are you going to draw?"

The little girl's eyes turned heavenward. "I know! I'll draw a fishy, like that one over there." She pointed to a dead fish, ripening on the beach.

The same one Sarah had been shooing Rex away from all morning. She exchanged glances with Frederick, trying not to let her true feelings about the smelly thing show and handed Alyssa the stick. "Oh, what a great idea!"

Rising off the ground, Sarah dusted sand off her filthy ragged skirt. She glanced down at Frederick. "I'm going to check on Mama. You stay here, and I'll bring back food for us." Frederick's wink and smile made her feel warm inside.

The drenched wood resulted in a smoky fire that made her cough when she got close to it, and she waved a hand to dispel the smoke.

"Sorry about that!" Mrs. Claiborne's cheerful voice was a joy to her ears in the midst of so much death, suffering, and disaster.

"At least it keeps the flies and mosquitoes at bay."

"You need something, honey?" Mama rubbed a bit of sand from Sarah's cheek while using her other hand to pat a slab of compressed corned beef with a spatula.

"I think we need to gather our family so we can talk about what we're going to do."

Mama cut the corned beef into slices and set each piece atop large crackers she pulled from one of the boxes marked *lighthouse rations*. One by one she handed them to Sarah, who stacked them in her hands. "I suppose we should get together and talk, but I have no idea what we'll do." She put the last beef-topped cracker on the stack leaning precariously against Sarah's chest and put her fists on her hips. "At least the Claibornes still have their house…for the most part anyway."

"What do I do with these?"

"Go hand them out. Save some back for yourself and the rest of the family. I'll come to you when I'm finished here."

"Thank you, Mama."

Grace joined Sarah in passing out the crackers and corned beef.

Guy and Frederick walked with them.

Guy held a pail of condensed milk mixed with rainwater, and Frederick carried a tin cup to distribute the milk or give out drinks when no vessel was available. The smell of food saturated the salty air. The weary storm survivors were very appreciative of the much-needed nourishment. By the time all had been served, the sun was high in the sky.

Mama wearily trudged to the place her family gathered.

"Thank you, Mrs. McKinney. This is wonderful," Frederick said.

"Yes, thank you, Mama." Sarah and Grace, in turn, gave their thanks.

Guy held his food up toward Mama "Thank you."

They had all waited for Mama to finish cooking before eating. Mama pulled the blanket back to see their precious newborn. She then settled on the ground, bending her legs to the side and pulling her skirt over them. "I wished y'all wouldn't have waited on me. Your food's probably all cold now!"

"It's fine, Mama. And thank you." Sarah held onto the last bite of meat and cracker even though she wanted to devour it. "Now that we have everyone all together we need to talk about ways to get off the peninsula."

"Well…" Grace looked at Guy. "Since we don't have a house anymore, and since Guy and me are betrothed to be married and all, the Claibornes have invited me to stay with them…here at the lighthouse." A sweet smile was shared between the young couple before Grace whipped her gaze back to Mama. "In separate rooms, of course!"

Mama rubbed her hands together; cracker crumbs fell to the sand. She closed her eyes and shook her head. "I don't have a problem with that since I don't have a home for you anyway." She shook a finger at Grace. "But only until I get settled!"

Grace snatched Guy up in a tight embrace and leaned her head against his chest. "I can live with that. Thank you, Mama."

Melvin stood and paced around amongst the

family. Raw emotions from the past few days became evident in his speech. "That takes care of them. Now, what about the rest of us?"

"Melvin, just calm down." Mama took Baby Melvin from Louise's arms before returning to her previous spot.

Frederick brushed cracker crumbs off his trousers and slipped his arm around Sarah's shoulder. She snuggled close to his side. "It seems we're in quite a pickle without the ferryboat to carry us off the peninsula."

"Has anyone been to the ferry landing to check?" Melvin asked.

"Yes. Some of the men walked the distance and reported the ferry as being destroyed," Frederick replied.

Louise gasped. "Destroyed?"

"Yes…one man recognized parts of the boat strewn about confirming their suspicions."

Mama rocked the sleeping baby in her arms. "We need to find a way to get over to Galveston."

"Mama, I looked out toward Galveston when we were all up in the lighthouse, and, and…" The words caught in her throat. She covered her mouth as tears swelled in her eyes.

"What is it, Sarah?"

"I think Galveston got hit much worse than we did. It looked bad, Mama—really bad." The memory of what she'd seen brought a stream of tears coursing down her cheeks.

Some of the other people gathered around heard what Sarah said. A low rumble of voices spread through the crowd.

"What did you see up there, miss?"

Frederick's strong arm clasped around her shoulder gave her strength. "It, it doesn't look like it did before. It looks like the whole island was poured into a big pail of water, swirled around, and then...poured back out." She pressed her face into Frederick's side.

Others frantically shouted questions.

Frederick held his hand up warding them off.

"Leave her alone! She doesn't know any more than the rest of us!" Mama's words stifled the shouting, and the crowd dispersed.

"Thank you, Mama."

"Listen." Melvin attempted a loud whisper. "Do you hear that?"

A faint sound roared in the distance.

Rex went on alert, twisting his head toward the sound.

The ship's horn sounded again.

"Should we go and have a look?" Frederick asked.

Sarah was already standing. "Yes, come on!"

They took off running toward what had once been the Bolivar ferry landing.

Rex ran along with them, barking all the way.

A huge barge headed into the strip of water that flowed between the Bolivar Peninsula and Galveston Island.

"Look, Frederick!" She pointed at the boat and started jumping up and down. She waved her arms wildly in the air.

The others followed her lead, whooping and hollering to get the attention of the barge's pilot. A chorus of voices shouted, their arms flailing about. "We're here! Help us! Over here! Over here!"

The barge continued on its course. A man

appeared on the barge's deck. He pulled off his cap and looked as though he were scratching his head.

"Look!" She shouted and pointed at the pilot.

Their yelling turned to screaming.

The man put his hat back on, turned away, and walked toward the pilothouse.

"Where's he going?" Sarah asked.

"I don't know, love. Surely he saw us." Frederick's fingers entwined with hers as they waited and watched. Frederick reached around, putting his hand on the back of her neck.

She looked up at the love of her life and received a warm kiss. Even though sadness hung thick in the air, Sarah was content as long as Frederick was by her side. She trusted him with her heart, her life, and her future. When the kiss had ended, Frederick touched the tip of her nose with his lips.

"Look," Frederick said.

The barge was heading toward the downed ferry landing.

"Oh, Frederick, we're saved."

A sly grin played on Frederick's face. "I should say this calls for another kiss."

Sarah's lips curled into a smile. She couldn't have agreed more.

39

Grace's embrace was so tight, Sarah could hardly speak. "Grace…Grace…you're choking me."

"I'm going to miss you all so much! Promise you'll send a wire once the lines are restored."

"I will. I promise." Sarah glanced around. "I think Mama wants to tell you goodbye."

Grace released her and ran sobbing in Mama's direction.

Frederick shook hands with Guy and his uncle.

She joined them in time to hear the man she loved pouring his heart out in thanks for protecting her and her family and for allowing him shelter. Sarah's heart swelled with pride, wondering why God would bless her with such an amazing man.

"Are you ready to go?" he asked.

"Ready as I'll ever be."

Hugs were shared, and tears were shed as Sarah and her family boarded the barge. She was sad to leave the peninsula. She cried a little at having to leave Rex behind. Daddy had given Rex to her when she was a little girl, and they'd been best friends ever since. It broke her heart to leave him with Grace and Guy. But they had no way of knowing what lay ahead of them, and Rex was safe at the lighthouse.

Before she got on the barge, Sarah looked into his big, brown eyes and tussled his thick hair. He put his paw on her arm and whined. She hugged him tight and whispered in his ear. "Don't worry, boy. I'll be back for you." She kissed his furry head and wiped away a tear.

Along with the sadness came a feeling of joyful anticipation for what God had in store for Frederick and her.

Forty-six other homeless storm survivors joined them on the barge. Some of their faces…their demeanors reminded Sarah of the old men she'd met who fought in the War Between the States. They had all been through something that no one should ever experience. And sadly, there was still so much uncertainty ahead.

The barge was bound for Galveston until word of the storm's destruction was received. All trade ships and barges were being diverted to the port at Texas City, where they were headed now. The mighty barge cut through the calm water leaving the past behind. Slowly they crept into Galveston Bay.

Sarah and Frederick sat on deck, and leaned against one of the many cargo containers onboard.

The water in the bay was practically unseen for all the debris blown off the island. Thousands upon thousands of boards and every conceivable object floated past. Traveling farther into the bay, Galveston Island came into plain sight from the barge.

Many who traveled with them wailed at what they saw.

"Where are all the buildings? I don't see any of the steeples. How can this be? It's…it's all gone!" Sarah gasped out.

"Yes, yes, I know. I'm so sorry, my dear, Sarah." He reached for her.

There was no way to make sense of the horror. She

couldn't look away from the destruction. Galveston, the wealthiest city in the entire state of Texas, lay in ruins. Buildings that once stretched to the sky stood as empty hulls. Beautiful mansions were reduced to endless piles of bricks and boards.

"I need some help over here!" A man stood close to the edge of the barge and shouted, drawing everyone's attention. Several men rushed to join him. He pointed into the water.

"What do you suppose that's all about?"

"I have no idea."

"I'll find out. You should stay here."

Sarah followed after Frederick.

The man who hollered for help was now lying on his stomach with his arms stretched out, grasping for something in the water. Frederick joined other men lying on the deck. They reached into the water and pulled one lifeless body after another from Galveston Bay.

Several women bawled at the horrific sight, and Sarah would have joined them, but there was no time for that. She needed to help. Kneeling on the deck beside Frederick, she reached into the water and firmly grasped the shirt of a young man.

"No! You shouldn't be here, Sarah!" Frederick said.

Her lips tightened into a straight line. Warding off the tears stinging her eyes had become a daunting task. "I can and I will! These are my people, and I'm going to help them." She turned back to the water and plunged her arms in, grabbing hold of another body.

Frederick helped her pull the dark-skinned woman on deck.

No more words were exchanged.

There were no words to adequately describe the horrific sight.

~*~

Frederick was more than relieved when the Texas City Port came into view. In the six and a half miles they'd traveled from the Bolivar Peninsula, the passengers and crew pulled forty bodies from the bay.

The barge pulled up to the dock.

His precious Sarah worked by his side the whole time without complaint. He would ask her to marry him, but not now, not here. His feelings for her were stronger than anything he'd ever experienced. She was all he'd ever wanted in a woman.

She caught him staring at her.

"I must look frightful." Sarah touched one of her long, blonde curls.

He nudged her chin up. "I've never seen you look more beautiful."

Sarah brought his hand to her lips and kissed it while looking into his eyes. "And you look very handsome wearing Daddy's hat."

Frederick inched the Stetson up on his head. "Well, I suppose we ought to do this." Taking Sarah by the hand, he led their way off the barge with the rest of her family.

Safely on land, Frederick turned back and looked at all the bodies littering the barge deck. How thankful he was that God had allowed them to survive the storm.

Sarah squeezed his hand.

The small town of Texas City, Texas was overrun with refugees from the island. Those who survived the storm were in a mass exodus from the island to towns farther north. Most had no home to return to. Joining the evacuees was a throng of manned carriages at the ready for anyone needing passage.

Frederick hoped Mr. Logan and his family had been able to leave the island before it was too late. But there was no use dwelling on things he had no control over.

"Sarah, Frederick. Come over here and let's talk." Melvin motioned them over to a low, decorative fence where Mrs. McKinney sat holding the baby. Louise sat next to her. The poor woman lacked color in her cheeks. She needed rest. Melvin looked at Frederick when he spoke. "It's time we regroup and come up with a plan." The man didn't look much better off than his wife.

It was time to take charge of the bedraggled crew. Frederick looked at Sarah's mother. "Mrs. McKinney, might I make a suggestion?"

"Well, of course you can. You have as much a say in what we do as any one of us."

"Why, thank you." He straightened his grubby shirt. "I think our best option is to travel to Houston to the home of your brother, my employer." Frederick paused to gauge her reaction. He gestured toward the carriage drivers. "I, I would like to ask a few of those gentlemen if anyone is heading toward Houston. If you are in agreement, of course."

"I suppose we don't have much other choice, son."

Frederick squeezed her hand. She smiled at him before they took off toward the rows of carriages. Mrs. McKinney had put her trust in him. She called him "son." He would do everything in his power to deserve the esteemed moniker.

40

Sarah's back ached. The wagon's wheels struck every rut, rock, and ravine on the road, and there was another hour's ride ahead of them. Glancing around, Sarah's family all looked uncomfortable, but Louise looked as if she was on her last bit of strength. At least the driver made good time in the forty-two miles between Texas City and Houston.

They weren't alone on the bumpy ride. The driver allowed two other families to join them in the wagon. No one dared complain about the cramped conditions. The wealthiest families were on the same level as the poor. There were none who hadn't suffered great losses. "Mama." Sarah reached over and tapped her mother's knee. "Mama, do you think Uncle Jeremiah will have received your wire by the time we arrive?"

"I don't know, honey. I just pray they're there and not in Galveston."

Sarah slumped back against the wagon's sidewall. She hadn't entertained the thought that they might not even be at their Houston ranch. Summer had passed; why would they still be in Galveston? "No. I don't think they would have been there."

"I pray you're right, honey."

Frederick whispered in Sarah's ear. "Don't worry, love. I'm sure they're fine."

She put both arms around Frederick's and squeezed tight. The excitement she felt about seeing her uncle and aunt quickly melted into a puddle of fear in the pit of her stomach. She closed her eyes, refusing to cry, and fell asleep clinging to Frederick's arm.

~*~

Sarah awakened with a start. She dreamed she was back in the lighthouse. It swayed back and forth so much that she'd fallen out and was trying to swim through rough storm waters. She hugged Frederick's arm still within her grasp, thankful it had only been a dream.

Uncle Jeremiah's ranch was up ahead.

The driver whipped the reins, and his team picked up the pace.

Uncle Jeremiah, Aunt Wilma, a half dozen hired hands, and a handful of grandchildren stood in the yard waving at them.

Relief washed over Sarah. She met Mama's gaze. "They're all right, Mama."

Her beleaguered mother attempted to smile. She closed her eyes and raised a hand toward heaven, her prayers obviously answered.

The driver stopped the wagon.

Everyone, including the two families who had joined them, climbed out of the wagon.

Sarah's uncle and all his family and workers met them halfway.

Mama collapsed into her brother's open arms.

Louise walked beside Melvin who held their newborn baby.

Aunt Wilma quickly made the connection. She gasped, put her hands to her cheeks, and then made a beeline toward the young family. "The baby has come!"

Before Melvin could protest, she whisked the tiny bundle from his hands. "Come, come now to the house. I need to take care of you."

Sarah was happy for someone to help her weary sister. She squeezed Frederick's hand.

Uncle Jeremiah patted Mama's back before letting her go. He walked toward Sarah and Frederick with his hand outstretched.

Frederick dropped Sarah's hand and wiped it off on his grubby pants before shaking his boss's hand.

Uncle Jeremiah put his other arm around Frederick's back and pulled him in for a hug, clapping his hand against his back. "I'm so glad to see you." Uncle Jeremiah released Frederick and took a long look at him. "The hat looks good on you, Son." He chuckled and then caught Sarah up in a bear hug. He kissed the top of her head. "Thank God you are all safe."

"And I thank God you weren't in Galveston."

His eyes revealed the sadness of what happened. He turned to the group of displaced Galvestonians. "You are all welcome to stay for dinner. My men are smoking briskets out back, and my wife is making a washtub full of potato salad. There's plenty for everyone."

A rousing round of thank yous and cries of joy came from the weary travelers and the wagon driver.

When Uncle Jeremiah headed toward the back yard, the people followed him.

~*~

Uncle Jeremiah's men cooked up quite a feast. Everyone ate until they hurt.

Thanking Uncle Jeremiah for the well-known Texas hospitality, the other two families loaded up in the wagon and took off. The driver refused to take the money Uncle Jeremiah offered him, saying the dinner was payment enough and that it was the least he could do after all they had been through.

Sarah would eventually go out to the pasture to see the breed stock she'd sent here months before. But for now, she was happy to sit on the big, wooden porch swing and listen to the birds sing. As long as she had Frederick by her side. He rubbed his thumb lightly across the back of her hand sending a ripple up her spine. The way he looked at her with those green eyes stirred her desire for him.

The screen door swung open wide, and Uncle Jeremiah, Mama, Aunt Wilma, and Melvin stepped out onto the porch. Each one of them held mugs of steaming coffee. Mama, Aunt Wilma and Melvin headed for the table and chairs. Melvin put his mug down and pulled out chairs for the women. Uncle Jeremiah leaned against the porch railing and took a long sip of his coffee.

Sarah sat up straight, hoping the blush on her cheeks would go unnoticed. "Mama, where are Louise and the baby?"

"Your Aunt Wilma took them to one of the spare bedrooms to sleep. Poor things were exhausted." An oppressive cloud of gloom seemed to surround her mother.

Sarah understood why, they had lost everything. But she couldn't forget that God had spared their lives.

Uncle Jeremiah looked at Frederick and smiled. "I can't believe you made it all the way from Beaumont to the lighthouse on Bolivar. The very place where Sarah was! Now that's true love."

Sarah took a sideways glance at her beau. He smiled, squeezing her hand.

"Yes, well I'm a man of my word. I told Sarah I would return for her and I did. I'll never leave her again."

Mama covered her face with her hands and sobbed.

Aunt Wilma put her arm around her shoulders to comfort her.

Sarah rose from the swing and went to her side. She pulled out the chair next to her and sat. "What is it, Mama?" Sarah took her mother's hands and pulled them away from her face.

Mama wiped her eyes and sucked in a gulping breath. "What are we going to do, Sarah? We lost everything…the house, the ranch, and everything in it. How much does God think I can handle? I've lost my three husbands—divorced one, and buried two. Now I don't have a husband. I don't have any money. I don't have anything! What am I supposed to do?"

Sarah's heart ached at the devastation in her mother's words. She took Mama's hands and squeezed them. "I know, Mama, but it'll be all right. Uncle Jeremiah said we could stay here."

"That's right. You are all welcome to stay for as long as you need to." Aunt Wilma tried her best to soothe Mama.

"And we have our lives, don't we? And you have Baby Melvin."

Mama smiled at the mention of her precious grandbaby.

"Mama, you know as well as anyone that God knew exactly what was going to happen to us.

And…He had everything figured out before the storm even formed in the Gulf."

Mama nodded in agreement.

"He's still on His throne, and He's still in control." Sarah gave Mama a sheepish grin. "You want to know how I know that?"

"What do you mean?"

Sarah stood and turned away from the men so they wouldn't see her reaching beneath her skirt. She fumbled a moment with the secret pocket hidden between the seams of the tattered garment until she had what she wanted. She sat back down beside Mama and placed the folded piece of paper in the palm of her hand. She closed Mama's fingers around it and let go with a big smile.

"What's this?"

"Well, open it up and see!"

Mama unfolded the thick paper.

"What is it?" Melvin asked, craning his neck to see.

Mama's hands began to shake. She started sobbing again, but this time were tears of joy. She reached out her other arm, and Sarah gladly fell into her embrace. The bank note waved to and fro in Mama's hand. Sarah never had the chance to do anything with the money she'd received from the sale of Papa's last herd.

Mama whispered in her ear. "You didn't spend the money."

"God knew we would need it more now."

"He has truly delivered us."

Sarah cried along with Mama, acknowledging the awesome power of God. An old, familiar verse came to her mind. She whispered it to Mama. "But my God shall supply all your needs according to His riches in glory by Christ Jesus."

"Yes, He does, baby girl. Yes, He does."

41

Sarah entered the parlor, supporting her back with her left hand. Her long, full skirt swished back and forth as she walked across the room to the desk situated in front of the side window. Carefully lowering herself into the desk chair, she took in a deep breath and released it. For a moment she stared at the tall stack of legal papers before softly chuckling. *Oh, Frederick…*

As difficult as it was, she managed to reach over the documents retrieving her journal from amongst Frederick's work. She pulled out the desk drawer and took one of the extravagant Waterman pens from its case. The beautiful matching set had been a wedding present from Louise and Melvin.

Opening the journal, she set pen to paper inking the date, Wednesday, June 5, 1901. She paused, relaxing her hand as she thought what to write. When nothing immediately came to mind, she used her most elegant curlicue penmanship to write the new name she was so proud to call her own. She was pleased with the results.

Sarah Jane Chessher.

Sarah startled when a sudden hiccup escaped her mouth. She giggled and put her hand atop her growing belly. "Your grandma would say, 'that baby is going to have a head full of hair!'" A smile graced Sarah's face thinking of Mama and how she swore by those old wives' tales. She missed Mama, but was happy to read in her latest letter about how she, Louise, and Melvin had put down money on a huge house in Bay City, Texas. Mama finally had her boardinghouse. Why she chose another place right on the Gulf of Mexico was a mystery to Sarah.

All three sisters and Mama kept in close contact. Grace's letters always made her laugh. Her stories about life in Tennessee with her preacher boy were hilarious. Their weekly letters were like a big slice of homemade pie. It was something to look forward to, something comfortable one really loved, like sleeping in one's own bed after a long trip. Sarah smiled. Turning her attention back to her journal, she wrote.

I've never been so happy in all my life. Feeling our baby move and knowing that he or she is growing inside me is the most wonderful sensation I've ever known. Never in my wildest dreams did I ever imagine I would love the life I have now. God has blessed Frederick and I beyond measure. I owe it all to the fact my husband now has his faith firmly planted in Jesus Christ as his Lord and Savior. I no longer worry. Thank You, God.

Who would have ever thought I would be happy in Beaumont, Texas? When Uncle Jeremiah suggested Frederick and I move here to open a second law office I wanted to cry. Turns out it was the best idea he ever had. Ever since those men struck oil on Spindletop Hill, people have been crawling out of the woodwork needing Frederick to file their legal claims.

Funny how things work out the way they do. All I know is that I love my Frederick and as long as I'm by his side my heart is content. I suppose that Bible verse is true. All things really do work together for good to them that love God and who are called according to His purpose.

Sarah set the pen on the desk and closed her journal. With one hand on her belly and her other hand on the edge of the chair, she stood—a task growing more difficult by the day. Moving toward the door, she remembered how Frederick teased her, accusing her of walking like a penguin. She had no idea how penguins walked, but imagined it must be much the same as how big bellied, pregnant women walked.

"Woof, woof, woof!" Rex bolted into the parlor.

Sarah went outside for fresh air around the same time every day, and he knew her routine. "Sit." Sarah gave the command as she removed Rex's lead from the coat hook where it hung.

Rex sat and waited while the leash was attached to his collar.

"Good boy, Rex." Sarah had promised to come back for him, and she kept her word. Opening the front door of their small house, Sarah breathed in the sweet smell of gardenias blooming outside their door. All the houses in town featured a quaint front porch. Even though Sarah knew more about raising cattle than she did about decorating, she had done her best to make the front of their home as inviting as possible. Sarah attached Rex's leash to the hook Frederick screwed into the wood railing. The dog made three complete circles before lying down on the porch.

Sarah sat at the charming little wrought iron conversation set that she and Frederick bought second hand and re-painted a crisp shade of yellow. A pot of bright pink petunias sat in the middle of the table. She plucked wilted flowers from the plant and off the tabletop and slipped them into her skirt pocket. With a contented smile, Sarah rubbed the round bump covering her middle. The baby was quiet now.

A man with a handlebar mustache and an expensive looking suit rode down the street on a beautiful brown and white paint. The clip-clop of hooves on the pavement tore at her heart. She missed Ginger in the worst way. But that part of her life was behind her…for now anyway.

"Hello, Sarah!"

Rex barked at the intruder, and Sarah looked up to see who was calling. "Oh, hello, Angela." She waved at the woman standing on the sidewalk in front of her house.

Sensing no threat, Rex put his head back down on the cool porch.

"Lovely weather we're having." The young woman took one hand off the baby carriage she was pushing to adjust the bonnet ribbon tied at her neck. "Albeit hot, though."

"Yes, I can attest to that." Sarah smiled, fanning herself with her hand. "And how is that little man of yours doing?"

The woman smiled at the tiny baby in her carriage. "He's perfect. You'll think the same thing when yours arrives."

Sarah placed her hand on her belly and laughed. "I'm sure I will!"

"Take care, Sarah."

"I will. Goodbye now."

Relaxing against the back of her chair, she observed the hustle and bustle of the big city of Beaumont. Having been raised on the Bolivar Peninsula, most any town was a big city to Sarah. Horse and buggies dashed down the busy street in front of their house. Telephone poles were going up all around town. Like Galveston had been prior to the storm, Beaumont was a forerunner for every sort of newfangled concept. How long before Frederick insisted they get a telephone in their home?

Sarah was overcome with apprehension before finally giving in to the idea of selling her breed stock to Uncle Jeremiah. It helped that he assured her he'd give her a hand should she ever decide to get back into ranching. But her decision to let go of that life and cling tight to the life God was offering her was such a liberating experience.

After all, it was God who divinely orchestrated every single event that brought Frederick and her together. And it was God who had been her refuge and her strong tower during one of the darkest days in Texas history. She was finished relying on her own strength in the storms of life. From now on she would put all her trust in Him—the Master of the Sea.

Rex's tail wagged, thumping on the porch boards.

She smiled, shaking her head at the silly dog. "Is he coming, Rex?"

He wagged harder. His bushy tail sounded like a straw broom hitting the porch.

"Don't worry, boy. He'll be home soon."

A glance down the sidewalk confirmed what Rex already knew. Sarah stood, and Rex jumped up. He barked and danced with excitement. The love of both their lives had arrived. How handsome he looked in his suit and tie, holding his overstuffed satchel by his side.

He winked at his mate. "Hello, Rex! Are you my good boy?" Frederick ruffled the dog's ears as he passed by. He dropped the satchel on a chair and pulled off his hat as he approached her.

Sarah adored how, even though she felt big as a

cow, he still looked at her as if she were a delicious bowl of strawberry ice cream. Frederick leaned in, grasping her face in his palms and passionately kissed her. His kisses would forever cause her temperature to rise.

"How is my little cowgirl today?"

Sarah blushed and fluttered her eyelashes. "I'm not a cowgirl. I'm the esteemed wife of a big city attorney."

Frederick smiled before bowing to her. "Why yes you are, my lady. And how is our little charge doing?"

She took his hand and placed it on her tight belly. "Just like you, perfect in every way."

Frederick took her hand in his and led her down the stairs to complete their evening routine. Taking Rex's leash, he offered his arm to her. "Madam?"

Sarah hooked arms with him. "Why, thank you, sir."

Pausing before beginning their walk, Frederick turned to look at his bride. "Mrs. Chessher, I understand you're not a cowgirl, but would you do me the honor of walking off into the sunset with me?"

Sarah looked up into her husband's big, emerald eyes. "Why, yes, I will, Mr. Chessher. Today and every day for as long as we both shall live."

Thank you

We appreciate you reading this White Rose Publishing title. For other inspirational stories, please visit our on-line bookstore at www.pelicanbookgroup.com.

For questions or more information, contact us at customer@pelicanbookgroup.com.

White Rose Publishing
Where Faith is the Cornerstone of Love™
an imprint of Pelican Book Group
www.PelicanBookGroup.com

Connect with Us
www.facebook.com/Pelicanbookgroup
www.twitter.com/pelicanbookgrp

To receive news and specials, subscribe to our bulletin
http://pelink.us/bulletin

May God's glory shine through
this inspirational work of fiction.

AMDG

You Can Help!

At Pelican Book Group it is our mission to entertain readers with fiction that uplifts the Gospel. It is our privilege to spend time with you awhile as you read our stories.

We believe you can help us to bring Christ into the lives of people across the globe. And you don't have to open your wallet or even leave your house!

Here are 3 simple things you can do to help us bring illuminating fiction™ to people everywhere.

1) If you enjoyed this book, write a positive review. Post it at online retailers and websites where readers gather. And share your review with us at reviews@pelicanbookgroup.com (this does give us permission to reprint your review in whole or in part.)

2) If you enjoyed this book, recommend it to a friend in person, at a book club or on social media.

3) If you have suggestions on how we can improve or expand our selection, let us know. We value your opinion. Use the contact form on our web site or e-mail us at customer@pelicanbookgroup.com

God Can Help!

Are you in need? The Almighty can do great things for you. Holy is His Name! He has mercy in every generation. He can lift up the lowly and accomplish all things. Reach out today.

Do not fear: I am with you; do not be anxious: I am your God. I will strengthen you, I will help you, I will uphold you with my victorious right hand.

~Isaiah 41:10 (NAB)

We pray daily, and we especially pray for everyone connected to Pelican Book Group—that includes you! If you have a specific need, we welcome the opportunity to pray for you. Share your needs or praise reports at http://pelink.us/pray4us

Free Book Offer

We're looking for booklovers like you to partner with us! Join our team of influencers today and periodically receive free eBooks and exclusive offers.

For more information
Visit http://pelicanbookgroup.com/booklovers